VICTORIAN
MANSION
FLOWER SHOP™
MYSTERIES™

The Mistletoe Murder

Lynette Sowell

AnniesFiction.com

Library of Congress-in-Publication Data
The Mistletoe Murder / by Lynette Sowell
p. cm.
I. Title
                    2017947647

AnniesFiction.com
(800) 282-6643
Victorian Mansion Flower Shop Mysteries™
Series Creators: Shari Lohner, Janice Tate
Series Editors: Janice Tate, Ken Tate
Cover Illustrator: Bill Bruning

10 11 12 13 14 | Printed in China | 9 8 7 6 5 4 3 2 1

1

The sound of Christmas music filtered into the study at Turtle Cove Mansion where Kaylee Bleu clutched several spools of velvety ribbon in shades of blue and silver. She smiled at the prospect of her design for this historic room, once a place where the gentleman of the house would entertain friends and perhaps enjoy a cigar or two. The room's austere tones would be brightened for Christmas, not in somber tones of red and green but in cheery blues and silver.

She could hardly wait to see it come to life.

Kaylee served on the committee for the House of Christmas Trees open house and auction, and she hoped their first event would be a resounding success. All the money raised—from ticket sales to tours of the century-old mansion to the auction of decorations and trees in each of the rooms—would go to a brand-new scholarship fund for local high school seniors.

She knew the value of a good education. She had been a plant taxonomy professor at the University of Washington in Seattle before she moved to Turtle Cove, Washington, with her loyal and inquisitive dachshund, Bear. When Kaylee lost her job due to cutbacks, she purchased The Flower Patch, her grandmother's shop, along with Wildflower Cottage, her grandmother's quaint farmhouse nestled in fields of lavender on Orcas Island.

Floral design was in her blood after learning the craft from her grandmother, Bea Lyons. So were plant taxonomy and botany, neither of which would come in handy while decorating a mansion for Christmas. But this event would let her show the island that The Flower Patch was in good hands with its new owner. Kaylee knew she had much to live up to, and she didn't want to disappoint her grandmother, now happily retired and basking in the Arizona sunshine with her sister.

She took a seat on the wingback chair and picked up a sketch pad, making notes as she did so. Pinecones, silver ferns. Another display with the *Euphorbia pulcherrima*, or poinsettias as most people called them, in a special shade of blue. Something for the mantel that could be removed and transported to a lucky bidder's home after the auction, which was in less than two weeks.

Laughter and chatter in the mansion's grand entryway clamored for her attention, but she ignored the noise. She preferred quiet while she was in design mode. Big personalities in small spaces didn't help fuel her creativity. But the mansion was plenty large enough for her and the other designers not to bump into each other . . . much.

At least she hoped so after last night's reception when she'd met the other designers. They had snacked on hors d'oeuvres and sipped punch while introducing themselves and sharing their ideas for their respective rooms in the mansion to the scholarship committee.

Kaylee wasn't sure who on the committee had recruited Duncan McTavish. She'd heard of temperamental designers, but Duncan's carefree, almost haphazard, ways were just as bad. Clad in a Hawaiian shirt and cargo shorts even though it was December, Duncan had arrived an hour late via skateboard, looking ready for a clambake. He pushed to the front of the line to describe his vision for his room, then said that he might not even execute that design because he didn't want to be predictable.

While Duncan made them laugh with some of his jokes, Kaylee didn't miss the thinly veiled exasperation a few others had for his antics. Rumor had it that he'd never finished high school, had wandered around various surfing competitions, then took up sand sculpting, and one day plunged headfirst into interior design.

Focus had also swirled around the arrival of Kristopher Carroll, a prominent designer in the Pacific Northwest. He had recently shot the pilot of *Celebrate with Kris*, his own cable TV design show. It was set to premiere this spring. The jovial man had a head of white hair with matching beard, and his booming laugh only lacked a "ho ho ho." Kaylee had seen Kris and fellow designer Barbara Lang-Masters out and about Orcas Island for several months, so she wasn't surprised he'd volunteered to design the grand entry hall of the mansion. The pair was inseparable throughout the evening, talking quietly and grinning at each other.

Barbara bragged about her more than two decades of design experience, and she emphasized that no one would see her designs for the immense dining room in the mansion until the very last moment. Despite Barbara's reputation as a diva, people raved about her designs for their vacation homes throughout the San Juan Islands. Kaylee suspected Barbara was counting on this open house and auction to boost her career beyond the islands and onto the mainland.

"Just get through the next two weeks," Kaylee kept telling herself. "It'll be good for the shop."

She held up three spools of ribbon to the orangey light of the study. Each shade definitely looked different than when viewed in the light at The Flower Patch's workroom. Good thing she'd brought all of them with her this morning. Her original choice of a grayish silver ribbon would appear almost brown in this light.

"Kaylee Bleu?"

She turned around as a camera flashed. She just knew she'd been caught with her mouth open. "Yes?"

"Mac Jordan, *Puget Sound Chronicle*." The bespectacled young man grinned. "I'm here to get a few photos of you designers in action for our preview piece."

"Thank you for coming," Kaylee said. An Orcas Island news reporter had spoken with the designers last night, and a reporter from the local newspaper had already interviewed them. Kaylee had been wondering if and when the rest of the media they'd invited would show up.

Mac glanced down at his camera screen. "Hmm, let's get a few more shots, shall we?"

Kaylee nodded. "Sure."

"How about you unwind some of the ribbons and pose by the fireplace as if you're planning an arrangement for the mantel?" he suggested.

"Good idea." Kaylee approached the mantel, a large beam of mahogany brought all the way from North Carolina a century ago. It would provide an excellent place for an evergreen bough covered with white LED mini-lights and festooned with blue ribbon. She hadn't decided whether to go with silver or white accents yet. Maybe that would be a last-minute decision, depending on whether there was a fresh blanket of snow on the ground on the day of the event.

Kaylee unspooled the ribbons, letting them billow in curls to the parquet floor. "There. How's that?" She held the ribbons up to the mantel and made a mental note to measure the width of the wood to see if it was wide enough to support evergreen branches.

Mac took a series of pictures. "Great. Do you know when Mr. Carroll will arrive?"

When the subject of the open house came up, everyone usually asked about Kristopher Carroll first. No wonder some of the other designers' egos were ruffled occasionally. None of them cared to share the spotlight, let alone see another designer be propelled to the front and center.

"No. But he should be here by now. We were supposed to arrive no later than nine." Kaylee smiled, trying to relax and look natural while the camera lens clicked. "His project is the grand entry hall."

Someone shouted in the entryway. And was that the honking of geese she heard?

"What on earth?" Kaylee glanced at the partially open study door.

A goat dashed into the study with a clatter of hooves. It rounded the wingback chair, then scampered past the fireplace, bleating. To Kaylee's astonishment, it snatched the other end of the dove-gray ribbon she held and yanked it from her hand. The thief scampered from the room, trailing the ribbon in its wake.

"Oh no you don't!" Tossing the remaining spools onto the seat of the other wingback chair by the fireplace, Kaylee scrambled to grab the spool bouncing along on the floor. She missed. It bounded through the open doorway.

Mac took pictures as he followed the goat.

This was *not* good. The House of Christmas Trees was the Turtle Cove committee's first attempt to raise funds for student scholarships, and pandemonium had broken out right in front of a member of the press, who seemed intent on documenting it. Whoever was responsible for this—

Kaylee skidded to a stop in the grand entryway, which at the moment looked like a combination of Old MacDonald's farm and a Victorian mansion halfway decorated for Christmas.

Swans—Kaylee counted seven of them—flapped their wings as they hopped along the double-sided staircase that wound up to the second floor along the entryway's rear wall.

The goat and her ribbon disappeared in the direction of the dining room, where Barbara's shrieking could be heard.

"Good heavens, this is not a *farm*!" Barbara exclaimed.

All the while, Duncan stood grinning beside the magnificent eighteen-foot artificial blue spruce in the center of the entryway. He thought this was funny?

"What is going on?" Mary Bishop—Kaylee's friend, part-time Flower Patch employee, and fellow Petal Pusher—emerged from the parlor as a dove landed on her shoulder. "Kaylee?"

"I have no idea." Kaylee glanced at the immense front doors. Then she noticed a camera crew from KSEA News 10 had set up a tripod and camera facing the entryway tree and Duncan. *Great, just great.* They managed to get a Seattle TV crew to the island, and now *this.*

Muddy footprints covered the floor. Someone would have quite a job cleaning all this up.

"Please tell me you're not filming this," Mary said to the young man sporting a tie and holding a microphone.

"Uh no, ma'am." The television reporter's eyes twinkled.

"We need to catch them and get them into the backyard where it's at least enclosed." Kaylee pounded up the stairs. She waved at the swans. "Shoo, get down from there. Get!"

Barbara strode into the entryway. She propped her hands on her hips. "Who is responsible for this melee? Who is feeding ribbon to a goat? And where is Kristopher?"

"That would be me feeding the goat. Unintentionally, I might add," Kaylee called down from the stairs. "I don't know where Mr. Carroll is."

"Kris is going to be late," Meghan Benson, Mr. Carroll's assistant, chimed in. "I'm not sure when he'll arrive. Last night at the reception he told me he wasn't feeling well and I should get started here without him." Her blonde hair swished past her shoulders as she waved both hands at a goose on the other staircase opposite Kaylee.

Kaylee didn't miss the sounds of *The Twelve Days of Christmas* that now boomed from an MP3 player's speakers resting on the coat-tree. She almost wanted to laugh, but for the swans who ignored her and decided that exploring the second-floor hallway off the staircase was more interesting than heading back downstairs.

It took a good ten minutes to round up the stampede that consisted of two doves, seven swans, six geese, three chickens, and the goat, which had managed to inhale half of the spool of Kaylee's ribbon before it darted outside.

Following it, Kaylee found a stack of cages that would hold the birds, and she let the others know about them.

All they needed was five rings and a pear tree. The goat could substitute for the partridge.

The goat now munched on wisps of dried grass in the backyard, which in summer was a kaleidoscope of color with its rose garden. Thankfully, roses weren't blooming now, although Kaylee mused that the hungry beast would probably snack on the thorn-covered branches. She'd heard somewhere that goats would devour entire rosebushes if given the chance.

When Kaylee arrived back in the entryway, she found Mary talking to the TV cameraman.

The young reporter looked sheepish as he folded his tripod. "I'm sorry. We had only about thirty minutes to shoot, and I just received another call I need to get to right away."

"We're the ones who are sorry." Kaylee glanced at Mary. "Is there any chance you might be able to come back another time? We'll be here working throughout the next two weeks."

The reporter shrugged. "I'm not sure. I'll try to put it on my schedule for Tuesday. But there's always the chance that something else might come up."

Kaylee knew her frown probably matched Mary's. "We understand."

Barbara tugged on the string of pearls around her neck, then smoothed strands from her gray bob over one ear. "This is not acceptable, simply not acceptable."

No, it wasn't really acceptable, but what could they do? Kaylee picked up a shred of ribbon. It was almost as though someone was trying to sabotage the event before they even started. Today's news clip would have been free publicity well beyond Turtle Cove and Orcas Island. But who would want to come when it looked like the committee didn't have anything under control?

The doors closed behind the news team, and the reporter made his apologies as well, promising to come back when the proverbial dust had settled.

"If Kris had seen this ridiculousness, he would have been livid." Meghan shook her head. "I should call him, let him know to brace himself for this. And who knows? Maybe his show's production company could pull some strings to get exposure for the open house and auction. Although I imagine their advertising budget is already spent." She pulled her phone from her pocket and hit a button.

The muffled sound of Beethoven's Ninth Symphony came from inside a storage closet tucked beneath the stairs, its door camouflaged to look like paneling.

"What in the world? That's his ringtone for me." Meghan sprinted over to the hidden door and opened it, then looked down at the floor and screamed.

Kaylee moved to Meghan's side and gazed down at Kris, who was lying on his back. He was dressed in a festive red polo shirt with a white collar, which was embroidered with holly leaves and darker berries on its pocket. She noticed two small splotches of red on his worn jeans.

"Call for help," Kaylee said to Meghan. "I'll check his breathing. I know CPR."

The young woman appeared frozen in place, but she snapped to attention when Kaylee touched her arm.

As Kaylee knelt over the motionless form in front of her, she didn't see any rise or fall of his chest nor any movement of his white beard or mustache to indicate breathing. His wire-rimmed glasses were still in place. She found no pulse.

Kristopher Carroll was dead.

2

This was a crime scene. It had to be. There was no other explanation as to why Kris lay in the storage closet, and Kaylee doubted he would have closed that door to shut himself inside. It was possible that he'd closed himself inside the closet, then had a medical emergency and been unable to use his phone, but it wasn't likely. The closet was not a place anyone would choose to hang out in. On the other hand, designers did odd things for inspiration. Maybe hiding in closets had been Kris's odd thing.

Kaylee pushed away her racing thoughts and sprang to her feet. "We have to step back. Nobody touch anything. We need to call the police."

"What's going on?" Barbara stumbled toward the closet. "Kris? What is he doing in that closet? Why didn't he tell us he was here already? I don't understand."

Mary took Barbara gently by the elbow. "Let's go sit down. I don't think there's anything you can do for him right now." She led Barbara through a nearby set of open pocket doors into the parlor.

Meghan paced the entryway. "This can't be happening. No, no, no." She leaned against the opposite stairwell, which also had a closet, and sank onto the floor. Then she rested her head on her knees, breathing deeply.

The next few minutes were a chaotic blur as an ambulance and a couple of deputies from the sheriff's department arrived at the same time. Deputy Nick Durham immediately cleared the entryway and announced that no one was permitted to leave the mansion until they were questioned. Except Barbara, who had collapsed. They sent for another ambulance to transport her to the Orcas Island Medical Center in Eastsound.

Everyone knew that Duncan was responsible for the animal circus. As soon as the police arrived, a van screeched to a halt in front of the mansion, and a man jumped out and retrieved the animals. In spite of the tragedy unfolding, it didn't escape anyone's notice when Duncan peeled some bills from his wallet and handed them to the animal handler, who muttered that he expected a tip. Few were amused by the prank.

Kris Carroll was pronounced dead at the scene, and the investigator took a series of photographs of the body and the closet and the surrounding area. Then the EMTs removed the body.

The designers anxiously waited in the parlor for their turn to be interviewed.

Nick stopped in the doorway, framed by pocket doors, and motioned to Kaylee.

She rose from the settee and joined him at the doors. "Deputy Durham."

"It's your turn." He led her into the very study she'd been prepared to decorate, which now served as the interview area.

Kaylee removed two spools of ribbon from the wingback chair before taking a seat across from Nick.

He got right to the point. "Obviously we have no confirmed cause of death yet, but I need your help in putting the pieces together."

"I understand. Whatever I can do to help, I will." Kaylee had nothing to worry about, but she still felt as if she was sitting in the principal's office.

"When was the last time you saw Mr. Carroll alive?" he asked.

She didn't have to think long about that. "It was at the reception last night. We—the designers—gathered for a meet and greet with the scholarship committee and the owner of the mansion. Everyone wanted to talk to Kris because of his new design show. It was supposed to premiere in the spring. It was a big deal."

"I see." Nick scribbled some notes. "Did you notice anything unusual, any odd interactions between him and any of the other guests?"

"No I didn't."

"So you didn't see Mr. Carroll this morning?"

"No. Mr. Carroll's assistant, Meghan, told us that he wasn't feeling well and he'd be late this morning. He wanted us to start working without him."

Nick nodded. "Very good. Did you have any interaction with him prior to the reception?"

"No, not really. I saw him a few times this fall when he picked up flowers, mainly roses, at The Flower Patch. He asked about the shop, and I told him about my grandma and how I'd bought it from her recently. I didn't learn much about him personally." Kaylee remembered how Kris had been kind and engaging, with an excited twinkle in his blue eyes that had made her feel as if she was the most interesting person he'd ever spoken to. She had noticed this in all his conversations.

Another nod from Nick. "Well, you're free to go. If you remember anything else from last night, anything unusual or that might be important—"

"I'll be sure to let you know," she finished for him, then rose from the chair.

"If you could, please send in Meghan Benson." He studied the notebook in his hand.

Kaylee reentered the parlor where the others waited. Meghan and Mary sat on an upholstered fainting couch, murmuring to each other. At one of the parlor windows, Duncan stood texting, his thumbs nimbly tapping on his phone. Kaylee approached Kris's assistant.

Meghan looked up. Her bloodshot, puffy eyes spoke volumes. "So it's my turn."

"Yes it is."

The young woman bit her lip, then fumbled with the crumpled tissue in her hands. "I've never had to talk to the police like this before. Am I in trouble?"

"No one's in trouble. At least not yet. Deputy Durham just wants to ask if you know anything about what might have happened to Mr. Carroll." Kaylee didn't want to say too much, but she believed that foul play was a strong possibility. Because Meghan had been Kris's assistant and had therefore spent more time with him than almost anyone, she would most likely be high on the list of suspects. Then again, any of them could be on that list, having been with Kris the night before he'd been found.

Meghan hesitated. Then she sucked in a deep breath and squared her shoulders. "I can do this."

"Yes you can," Kaylee said. "No one's been accused of anything."

Yet. The word hung unspoken in the air, as clearly as if she'd said it out loud.

Meghan nodded and strode from the room, the heels of her knee-high boots making determined clicks on the parquet floor.

Mary shook her head. "Unbelievable, just unbelievable."

"I know. Poor Kris." Kaylee dropped next to Mary on the couch. She let out a puff of breath. Then she thought of Sierra Underwood, the House of Christmas Trees committee chairwoman. Sierra was a loyal customer of The Flower Patch, and she had invited Kaylee to join the committee. The two had become fast friends since then. "Did anyone let Sierra know?"

"I've already called her," Mary answered. "The planning

committee is going to hold an emergency meeting on how to proceed with the open house."

Kaylee looked through the doorway at the muddied entryway tiles. Someone would need to clean up the muddy tracks the livestock and poultry had made all over the floors. "I don't think we'll be able to clean up the mess in that entryway anytime soon. No telling how long they'll be collecting evidence."

"No thanks to him," Mary hissed under her breath. She glared at Duncan, still entranced with his phone and lost in his own little world.

"I'm already trying to figure out how Kris could have ended up in that closet," Kaylee whispered.

"Yes, me too." Mary also lowered her voice. "The other Petals want to meet for coffee ASAP."

The Petal Pushers garden club shared a passion for all things floral and green, and it was one of the best parts of Kaylee's life in Turtle Cove. When Kaylee moved to the island amid the tumultuous changes in her professional life, they'd accepted her into their merry band as a replacement for their beloved Bea Lyons, Kaylee's grandmother. Their meetings contained discussions about life and love as well as actual gardening.

"I called Jess," Mary continued, "and she asked DeeDee to meet us at Death by Chocolate."

Jessica Roberts and DeeDee Wilcox were the other members of the Petal Pushers, and they couldn't resist a good mystery. Jessica owned the bakery and coffee shop where they often gathered.

"We can head over there as soon as you're done talking to Nick."

"You don't need to wait for me," Mary said. "Get a head start on that cup of coffee."

Before Kaylee could say anything else, Meghan strode back into the parlor.

"He's ready to see you now, Mary," she announced. Her eyes were overbright, but her voice was even. She removed her keys from her shoulder bag and darted from the parlor almost as quickly as she'd entered.

Mary stood, tugging at the hem of her coat, and turned to Kaylee. "I'll meet you at the bakery as soon as I'm done here."

"See you in a bit."

"Guess they're saving the best for last," Duncan quipped when it was just Kaylee and him in the parlor.

Kaylee didn't know how to respond, although she felt like saying a more appropriate description would be that they were saving the biggest ego for last. Now it was her turn to stand and gaze out one of the large-paned windows that gave a peek of the gray harbor beyond the neighboring rooftops.

"Look, the thing with the animals was a joke," Duncan said. "Plain and simple. I didn't plan for it to rain overnight, so that mess was completely unintentional. It's not like I was out to hurt anyone, especially Kris."

She looked at him sharply. "Who said anyone hurt Kris?"

Duncan shrugged. "Well, you got all Jessica Fletcher when Meghan opened the closet door, so it seems like you think foul play was involved."

"I don't know if it was or not, but of course the police need to find out how he wound up in that closet." Kaylee narrowed her eyes. "It's usually customary to investigate an unattended death if there's a chance it could be foul play. Since Deputy Durham is taking the time to question all of us himself, it looks like I'm not the only one wondering the same thing."

"Touché."

"So where were you last night after the reception?" Kaylee asked.

"Everything was already shut down here so I went to

Eastsound. I found a pub and stayed till closing. I'm going to tell the nice deputy that he can ask anyone." Duncan gave her an even look. "Where were *you* last night?"

"At home with my dog."

"No alibi. That doesn't bode well for you, does it?"

Kaylee tried not to roll her eyes.

Drops of rain began to patter on the windows, and they fit Kaylee's mood just fine. She needed that cup of coffee an hour ago. She would hear if the designers or committee members needed her help cleaning up the sorry mess at the mansion as soon as the police department cleared the premises.

Kaylee grabbed her purse and headed into the light rain.

Jessica had just handed a cup of coffee to a customer when Kaylee walked into Death by Chocolate.

"Kaylee, are you all right?" her friend asked, racing around the counter to hug her.

"Yes." Kaylee relaxed for the first time in hours, inhaling the aroma of freshly brewed coffee and ground beans. The rich smell of chocolate hung in the air too, along with the buttery scent of pastries. Her stomach growled. She'd been in a hurry to get out the door this morning and hadn't grabbed anything to eat.

Jessica made for the pot behind the counter. "Here. This one's on the house. And I'm adding an extra shot of espresso," she said, pouring a cup of coffee and sliding it across the antique wooden counter. "I couldn't believe it when Mary told me about Mr. Carroll."

Kaylee nodded. "I'm still in shock." She couldn't get the image of Kris lying there on the closet floor out of her head.

"I should have known there was a tragedy. Oliver has been droopy and pensive since yesterday." Jessica pointed at a potted lavender geranium on the counter, which she'd dubbed Oliver. She interpreted any sudden droopiness or loss of petals as a harbinger of bad things to come for someone in Turtle Cove.

Despite the terrible situation, Kaylee hid a smile as she lifted the cup and took a sip. "Mary will be here soon."

"DeeDee is on her way too." Jessica bit her lip. "This is awful, just awful. Poor Mr. Carroll, passing away so close to Christmas."

A few minutes later the lone customer left the shop just as Mary and DeeDee entered together.

Mary shook the rain off her umbrella before tucking it into the stand by the door. "Kris Carroll was so young. Only fifty-five. *Fifty-five.* It's hard to believe."

Jessica fetched cups of coffee for the newcomers, and the four women settled around the table closest to the counter.

"So what do you think happened to Mr. Carroll? A medical emergency?" DeeDee asked.

"Maybe. I wonder if he had any medical issues," Kaylee said. "Meghan, his assistant, would know."

"Who do you think was the last person to talk to him?" Mary said.

"I bet it was Barbara," Jessica said, eyes bright. "For the last few months she was either with Kris or talking about him every time she stopped in here. Was she at the mansion this morning?"

"Yes, she was in the dining room, working on her design," Mary replied.

"I'm glad she wasn't the one who opened the closet door," Kaylee said. "It was awful."

Besides seeing Kris lying there in the closet, Barbara's sobs had been the saddest thing this morning. The recollection brought a lump to Kaylee's throat, making her think of how her grandmother must have felt when she'd learned of her husband's passing. She pushed those thoughts aside, forcing herself to focus on her grandmother's current happiness with her sister.

"Maybe it was just an accident," DeeDee suggested. "Perhaps he hit his head on something in the closet and knocked himself out."

"That wouldn't have killed him, though," Jessica pointed out.

"I don't know," Kaylee said. "I didn't notice any evident injuries. I saw a couple of red splotches on his jeans, but I'm not positive it was blood."

"Maybe somebody moved his body from somewhere else and stuck it in the closet," Jessica offered.

Mary shuddered. "Oh my."

"That's a possibility. I mean, where would you hide a body on Orcas Island anyway?" Kaylee wondered aloud. "But why in the mansion?"

Jessica took a sip of her coffee, then set the cup down. "I'm concerned with *who* could have wanted to hurt him. He's a popular man, and everyone's been talking about his new show. It's going to be an instant hit. Or it would have been an instant hit."

Kaylee noticed worry lines on Mary's forehead. "What is it?"

"Well, I saw something odd at the reception last night. It might be nothing." Mary bit her lower lip. "I've been thinking about it ever since I heard the news."

"Come on." DeeDee nudged Mary's elbow. "Spit it out."

"While everyone was mixing and mingling, I saw Kris over in a corner, talking to Sierra Underwood, who chairs the committee. It didn't look like a good conversation either."

"How so?" Kaylee asked.

"Neither of them appeared happy. In fact, Kris looked angry—his cheeks were red—and when Sierra tried to walk away from him, he grabbed her arm and she pulled away." Mary frowned. "It didn't look like he grabbed her arm very hard, but still . . ."

Silence hung between the four of them for a few moments.

DeeDee broke the silence. "Just because they had a disagreement or a heated conversation doesn't mean one of them wanted to hurt the other."

"That's true enough," Kaylee agreed. Maybe it had a perfectly simple explanation, like DeeDee suggested.

"The House of Christmas Trees committee will be meeting soon. One of us should take Sierra aside and see what she says about it." Mary turned to Kaylee. "You seem a bit closer to her than the rest of us. How about you talk to her?"

"Sure. But I don't know if what she has to say will have any bearing on what happened to Kris."

At least, I hope it doesn't.

3

Later that afternoon Kaylee and Mary returned to The Flower Patch. A steady rain continued to beat down outside. The gloomy weather mirrored everyone's mood.

The House of Christmas Trees committee was planning to hold a meeting at the shop that afternoon. While she waited for everyone to arrive, Kaylee processed online orders. Mary swept the sales floor and put together Christmas-themed baskets with locally handmade artisan candles and DeeDee's handcrafted lavender goat milk soap. DeeDee owned Between the Lines bookshop across the street, and she was also a talented soap maker. Kaylee was thrilled to offer DeeDee's creations at her own store.

Mary slipped the last basket into a clear plastic bag, then tied a ribbon around the top. "There. Ready for giving," she announced as Kaylee entered the workroom.

"Perfect." Kaylee nodded at the gift baskets. They had practically flown off the shelves ever since Kaylee had put them up for sale beginning after Thanksgiving on Black Friday.

Her six-year-old dachshund, Bear, trotted after her and plopped down at her feet. The little dog had been her faithful, floppy-eared shadow since she'd adopted him from a shelter as a puppy, trying to carry a chew toy that was almost as big as he was. He had grown into a cute, curious dog, who seemed to be a good judge of character, and Kaylee suspected that he enjoyed wearing bow ties and other outfits as much as she enjoyed putting them on him. Today Bear sported a blue bow tie with little white bones on it. She thought he looked particularly dapper in it.

The bell over the front door chimed, and Bear scampered toward it, yipping gleefully.

Kaylee followed and greeted Sierra at the door. She noticed the woman's eyes were puffy, the whites of her eyes tinted a faint pink. Kaylee shushed Bear, who quieted immediately as if sensing the other woman's distress. "I'm glad you made it. How are you holding up?" she asked as she led Sierra to the consultation area. Kaylee waved at Mary as she passed, signaling that she would want to be in on the conversation as well.

"I'm doing okay." Sierra gave her a thin smile before settling onto the love seat.

Bear sat at Sierra's feet, pressing his small body against her legs.

Good boy, Bear.

Mary joined them just as the rest of the committee descended on the shop. All but Barbara Lang-Masters, but they weren't expecting her after what had happened this morning and her subsequent trip to the hospital.

Sierra took a deep breath and opened her notebook. "Considering the death of Mr. Carroll, I'd like for us to figure out a plan to forge ahead with the House of Christmas Trees. This was something Mr. Carroll felt very strongly about, and I know he'd want us to continue. That being said, out of respect for him . . ." She swallowed hard.

The others waited for her to go on.

"Out of respect for him, I think we should postpone the open house. His design was one of the most advertised parts of our show, so we need to decide on whether or not to include it."

"I think that would also be up to Meghan," Mary interjected. "She might need assistance to install everything."

"I don't mind helping Meghan," Kaylee said. "I think it's important that Mr. Carroll's design be seen by everyone. Especially if the draw for this event will help with scholarships for the students."

"What about Barbara?" Mary asked. "Has anyone heard from her?"

Sierra made a face at the mention of Barbara's name.

What's that about? "I tried her cell phone and only reached her voice mail," Kaylee said, "but I imagine she might still be at the hospital. I hope she's all right."

"I think we should take a vote now," Sierra said. "We have a committee majority here. I don't see the need to wait for Barbara."

They took a quick vote and unanimously approved keeping Kris's design in the plan. They followed that with a vote for Kaylee to help Meghan with the design if needed.

"Meghan was pretty upset this morning and understandably so," Kaylee said. "I know she's worked with Kris since she completed an internship after design school. She mentioned it at the reception last night."

The bell over the front door chimed. Barbara entered, her expression as gray as the afternoon outside.

"You're here." Mary rose and went to Barbara's side. "You didn't need to be."

"Yes I do." Barbara's voice held an unmistakable quaver. "The ER physician said I'm fine. I took a pill for my nerves, so I hope I don't get too sleepy."

"Barbara, it's all right. Please go home and get some rest," Sierra said. "One of us can drive you. We can continue our meeting without you. We know you and Mr. Carroll had become very close."

"No!" Barbara snapped. She glared at Sierra, her blue eyes crackling with heat. "No one is making any decisions here without me. I'm staying. Making sure Kris's work is seen by everyone is the most important thing to me right now."

Everyone gaped at her outburst.

Barbara burst into tears and sank onto an empty ottoman. "I'm so sorry. The day has been indescribably rough. I'm yelling at people over nothing, and I just don't know what to do." She pulled a tissue from her purse and dabbed at her eyes. "Kris—there's no easy way to say this, but we were planning to get married. This spring. It was his favorite season."

"Oh, Barbara," Mary said. "We had no idea."

Barbara nodded. "We agreed to keep our relationship quiet. And then things happened so fast between us this fall. We were going to announce our engagement at the open house." She began crying again and lifted her hand to her mouth.

For the first time, Kaylee noticed a sparkling ring on Barbara's left hand. A brilliant-cut diamond was surrounded by sapphires and set in a white-gold band. Kaylee guessed it was around two carats.

"So that's why Mr. Carroll was spending so much time on Orcas Island," Kaylee remarked. "I figured he just liked the weekend getaways."

Barbara nodded, twisting her pearl necklace around one finger. "It was like a beautiful dream, the two of us together. But none of that matters now."

"I'm very sorry," Mary said, leaning over and laying a hand on Barbara's shoulder.

Barbara touched Mary's hand. "Well, we will go on. We must go on. Kristopher would want it. His final design for the students of Orcas Island—" She broke off.

"I know." Sierra's voice was scarcely above a whisper. "He was ecstatic about what the funds would mean for the kids, especially those who need scholarships to continue their education."

Kaylee knew Sierra spoke from personal experience. The young woman had told Kaylee that she'd become a CPA thanks to scholarships. Her mother, who'd raised Sierra alone, hadn't been able to pay for her college. Sierra had been very close with her mother, who'd passed away the previous summer after battling cancer for several years. Sierra had been by her side the entire time.

Barbara let out a deep sigh. "And what will become of his show? The pilot hasn't even aired yet."

"It's too early to know what will happen with that. The production company will know how to handle it," the ever-practical Mary assured her. "But what about his family? Does he have any relatives nearby?"

"Not really. He might have a brother somewhere on the East Coast, but Kris wasn't even sure if he was still alive. Their parents are long gone." Barbara licked her lips. "We hadn't talked about families much. Just design and beautiful things. He made the most mundane, ordinary things sparkle. Every moment with him was a gift. Connecting with him was . . . indescribable."

Someone's phone buzzed. They all looked around.

Sierra held up her phone. "I'm sorry, but I need to take this call. As soon as the police are finished investigating, I'll let you know when we can access the mansion again."

"When do you think that'll be?" Kaylee asked.

"Deputy Durham said it shouldn't be too much longer. Maybe we can get back inside the mansion by tomorrow morning or afternoon." Sierra stood, slinging her purse strap over her shoulder and closing her notebook with a snap. "Well, I need to get going."

"Don't you worry. We'll get right back on track with the open house planning and honoring Mr. Carroll," Mary said.

Sierra nodded and strode out of the shop.

"What? Have plans been made already?" Barbara demanded, her voice leaping at least an octave.

"No, no concrete plans." Mary's tone was bright, upbeat, nonconfrontational. Kaylee didn't know how Mary did it sometimes.

"I'm going to speak with Meghan to see if she'd like help completing Kris's display. That is, if she's planning to stay to complete the job." Kaylee realized none of them had actually talked to Kris's assistant yet. Everything they'd just discussed might be premature.

"What if she pulls out and leaves?" Mary asked. "She's under no obligation to stay. And surely someone will need to see to Kris's legal and financial affairs, not to mention arrangements. I guess that'll fall to her, given his lack of family."

"I'll help her with that," Barbara said. "I'm glad the open house will continue. Right now, it feels like everything is going to happen fast, and my dear Kristopher isn't even buried."

"I can't imagine what a shock this must be for you." Kaylee noted fresh tears in Barbara's eyes. "If you need anything, we'll be glad to pitch in."

"Thank you." Barbara rose, smoothing the front of her pants. "I'll keep myself busy with my work and trying to think of what Kris would want."

Mary nodded. "We'll all think of that. In the meantime, I know we have plenty to do. If one of us hears from Sierra, text the others and we can meet again."

Kaylee and Mary watched as Barbara and the rest of the committee silently left the shop. It was quiet except for the sound of Bear's snore nearby. He'd fallen asleep against a nearby chair, and Kaylee wondered when he'd moved.

"Well, that's it for now." Kaylee faced Mary. "As you said, we have plenty of work to do. I'm heading upstairs."

The bell over the front door rang.

At the sound, Bear jolted awake and barked once.

Mary went to greet the customer, and Kaylee scaled the stairs, the sound of Bear's little paws following her. She immersed herself in making bows and arrangements until it was time to close for the day.

"Go home," Kaylee told Mary. "I'm sure Herb is anxious to see you after this morning."

"Thanks. I'll see you bright and early." Mary grabbed her coat and purse and left.

As Kaylee shut things down for the night, she thought about Kris's untimely death. She decided that a call to her grandmother was in order when she got home. Nothing soothed her like her grandmother's wisdom and warmth.

And she needed to hear her grandmother's comforting words tonight more than ever.

Kaylee was halfway through a cup of coffee the following morning when her phone rang.

Deputy Nick Durham sounded rather insistent. "Could you please come to the station as soon as possible this morning? I need your botany expertise regarding Mr. Carroll's case. I'm sorry for the short notice, but the sooner the better."

Prior to moving to Orcas Island, Kaylee had consulted as a forensic botanist in the Seattle area, but most of the time she examined evidence collected from crimes with a microscope. She'd been to just one or two crime scenes in the past, and her only responsibilities had been identifying plants and vegetation, not investigating. Kaylee had offered her services to Sheriff Maddox on previous cases, and she welcomed the chance to help out again.

"Of course. I'll be there within the hour." She wanted to ask him more, but her questions could wait. The fact that Nick had referred to it as a case—and hadn't flirted with her on the phone—told her plenty.

Her suspicion that Kris Carroll had met his end by foul play ratcheted up a notch. She wondered who had alibis and who didn't.

Kaylee looked down at the little dachshund at her feet. "Bear, do you want to go to the sheriff's department with me?"

In response, the dog jumped up and wagged his tail.

She laughed and patted his head. "I'll take that as a yes."

It wasn't long before they had made the short drive to Eastsound. As Kaylee carried Bear, wearing a bow tie with red and white stripes, into the Orcas Island Police Department, she immediately caught a whiff of wintergreen.

Aida Friedman sat at the reception desk, popping a couple of Tic Tacs into her mouth. The receptionist had a pack-a-day habit, which always made the office smell minty. Her light blue eyes and fair skin were accented by her designer glasses. She grinned at Kaylee and reached out to scratch behind Bear's ears. "What brings you two here today?"

"I have a meeting with Deputy Durham."

"I'll let him know you're here." Aida stood. "Do you need some coffee? I'm on my fourth cup. Or is it my fifth? I can't remember. Well, anyway, I can grab you some."

Kaylee hid a grin at Aida's caffeine-fueled rambling. "That would be great. Thank you."

As Aida bustled off, Kaylee realized she hadn't had a chance to let her know she'd like one cream and one sugar. She'd seen how Aida doctored her own coffee.

A minute later, Aida burst back into the reception area and handed Kaylee a cup of coffee. "I let Nick know you're here.

He'll be with you in a moment." As she returned to her desk, she added, "By the way, you missed your chance with him."

Kaylee sighed. Aida had tried to convince her to go out with the deputy, who had a reputation as a major flirt when he was off-duty and had even asked Kaylee to dinner a few times in her first months on Orcas Island. Lately, though, he'd stopped flirting with her and had just been friendly, and she was grateful for the change in attitude.

"Yeah, he's going after the new hairdresser now," Aida continued, clearly misinterpreting Kaylee's reaction. "I've never seen him be so regular about haircuts. And apparently *she* actually gives him the time of day," she said accusingly. "They've been on several dates, and they really seem to like each other."

"I wish them all the happiness in the world," Kaylee replied honestly. She took a sip of coffee. It was good but strong, and the sweetness made at least one tooth shriek with threatened decay.

Deputy Durham stuck his head through the doorway and waved to her. "Hey, Kaylee. Come on back."

Kaylee nodded.

"I'll see you soon at the shop," Aida told her. The receptionist was a regular customer at The Flower Patch. She stopped by every week to buy an assortment of dyed carnations, and she always brought Bear a treat.

"Great. See you later," Kaylee said, then headed into the private office area, with Bear ambling along beside her.

Nick led her down the hall to his office. "Thanks for coming. Again, I'm sorry for the short notice, but we need to get some answers as soon as possible. You understand the time crunch we work under." He closed the door, sat down behind his desk, and motioned for her to take a seat.

"Of course. It's no problem." She settled onto a worn chair that had seen better days.

Bear sat alertly in her lap.

"All right. We haven't released this yet, but I think it's important you know. Kristopher Carroll didn't die in that closet. Giles Akin hasn't quite nailed down the time of death yet, but judging by the body, he believes Mr. Carroll died somewhere else and was moved to that location, which is why there wasn't much blood. He'd also been shot."

Kaylee gasped. Her mind reeled from the idea of someone shooting such a jovial man.

"So this is the tangle we face," Nick went on. "If the bullet didn't kill him, what did? It will take time for the initial toxicology screens to come back, even though we've put a rush on them."

"How can I help?" Kaylee asked.

"Right now we need to get to work on the evidence we do have. We're hoping you'll help us discover where Mr. Carroll was when he died. We initially didn't find any mud on his boots."

She nodded, the pieces fitting together in her mind. "And the night before last, it rained but not until early that morning. I don't remember the entryway being muddy, if someone dragged him into the mansion. Maybe it was before it rained."

"There are no tracks, no marks," Nick added. "It didn't start raining until about four in the morning, so we think he was put in the closet before then."

"And if there were any tracks or marks on the floor, the animals let loose at the mansion took care of anything in the entryway." Kaylee frowned. "How convenient that Duncan McTavish unleashed such bedlam the next morning."

"Exactly." Nick leaned back in his chair. "We've started to pull some vegetation samples from Mr. Carroll's clothing and boots, as well as any traces found on the closet floor. Everything else in the entryway has been contaminated."

"Where are the samples?"

"Akin Funeral Chapel. Mr. Akin's been designated as a deputy by the medical examiner's office. He's collecting samples, and we can make much faster progress if you take a look at what we have so far."

"I don't know how helpful the samples will be. There's not much blooming in the winter, but the grass and soil should be able to tell us something. Of course I won't know for sure until I look."

A knock sounded on the door.

Nick raised his voice. "Come in."

Another deputy ducked into the room. "Miss Benson's here, and Robyn's about to interview her."

"Thanks. Be right there," Nick said, then turned to Kaylee. "How well do you know Meghan Benson?"

"Not very well. I met her only a couple of days ago."

Nick stood. "I've asked her to come in and tell me if she's thought of anyone who might have wanted to harm Mr. Carroll. She has no alibi."

"I see."

"Miss Benson might shed some light on where Mr. Carroll was the evening after the reception. She, out of anyone, should be able to tell us more about Mr. Carroll's interactions leading up to his death. This might be of some help to you as well. Come with me."

Kaylee scooped up Bear and followed Nick to a small room down the hall.

One wall inside the room featured a two-way mirror that showed an interview room next door. Kaylee looked through the mirror and saw Meghan seated at a square wooden table. Kris's assistant appeared every inch the professional, but her eyes had fine lines around them and dark circles underneath that her makeup didn't quite conceal.

Across from Meghan sat Deputy Robyn Garcia. She wore her light brown hair in her usual ponytail. "How long did you know Mr. Carroll?" she asked.

"I've known—I knew Kris for about six years." Meghan's voice came through a speaker. "I landed an internship with his company not long after I finished design school. It was the opportunity of a lifetime. I've been with Carroll Design ever since. I-I learned so much from him." Her eyes filled, and she wiped at them.

Robyn grabbed a box of tissues from the table and handed it to Meghan. "At the reception, Mr. Carroll said that he wasn't feeling well and planned to arrive at the mansion late the next morning. Around what time did he tell you that?"

"About eight thirty, I think. The big clock in the foyer had just chimed a half hour, and I remember thinking it was pretty early for Kris to leave a party. For a guy in his fifties, he sure had a lot of energy. He was a night owl. There were times he'd text me after midnight with an idea he'd just come up with."

Robyn jotted down notes. "Was anyone around? Did anyone else hear Mr. Carroll tell you how he felt?"

"There were many people around. Well, the scholarship committee, us designers, a guy from the local paper. I don't know if anyone else heard what he told me, but I wouldn't be surprised."

Kaylee thought back to the reception. Yes, there'd been many people. But what if the photographer from the newspaper had taken some photos? Or anyone else for that matter? When did Kris leave? Were there signs at the reception that he was sick? She didn't remember seeing any.

"Did Mr. Carroll talk to you about any health problems?" Robyn asked.

"He didn't mention anything other than his back and knees

bothering him sometimes. It made getting up and down stepladders a little tricky, which is why he started having me do that." Meghan smiled. "He said he wanted someone younger and faster to take over for him."

Robyn stopped scribbling. "He was leaving the business to you?"

Meghan shrugged. "If that was the plan, he never told me. I think he was going to have someone younger travel as the face of the company so he could stay in the office, except to film the show. He always said they'd have to carry him away from his design board. He was old school and liked to sketch everything out by hand instead of designing on a computer."

"How were things at the office during the last few months?"

"Very difficult." Meghan's voice quavered. "With Kris spending so much time here on the island, I was managing the office as best I could and reporting to him here every week. But he was head over heels in love with Barbara, and I don't begrudge him that time. I'd never seen him so happy."

"We've spoken to Barbara too," Robyn said. "But I'll still need a list of everyone else who worked with him, especially those who worked with him recently."

"We have a small office. There's just a receptionist and me." Meghan stared at the deputy. "Do you think someone murdered Kris?"

"Right now, we're piecing things together. Maybe he went back to the mansion later that evening and had a medical emergency. It's all still preliminary."

Meghan nodded. "I'll help however I can."

At the end of the interview Robyn asked Meghan not to leave the island without notifying the office and to let the police know immediately if she thought of anything else that might help shed some light on Mr. Carroll's last moments.

Nick escorted Kaylee to the reception area. "Thanks again for agreeing to help. Mr. Akin will be in touch with you when he finishes collecting samples. Then you can have free rein to examine whatever you need."

"I'll be ready," Kaylee said.

She said good-bye to Nick and Aida and carried Bear out of the sheriff's department. Before she reached her Escape, her phone rang.

She could hardly understand Barbara on the other end of the line. "What's that? I'm sorry. I don't know what you're saying."

The sound of Barbara's shuddering breath came through the phone, and when she tried again, her voice shook. "You need to come to the mansion right away. Someone's ruined everything."

4

Between sobs and broken sentences from Barbara, Kaylee gathered that someone had broken into the mansion and destroyed the Christmas displays that had already been set up. The mansion held tours and sometimes private events throughout the year. This holiday season, a few decorations had been put up in anticipation of the open house.

She dropped Bear off at home and gave him a treat, then raced to the mansion to join the group that had gathered in the entry hall. The muddy footprints tracked in by the animals yesterday remained on the floor, along with the tatters of the crime scene tape that had been up the previous day.

Deputy Durham arrived right behind Kaylee to inspect the damage.

"It's not the building itself, thank goodness," Barbara said. "But all the designers' work so far—the Christmas trees! Just look."

"Who discovered the intrusion?" Nick asked.

"That would be me," Sierra announced. "I picked up the key from the property manager's office this morning and stopped by to see what I could do to clean up the mess the animals made. I found the front door ajar and all . . . this." She gestured at the mess.

"Have you spoken to the owner of the mansion about the break-in yet?"

"Yes, the owner wants a thorough inspection and cataloging of the furniture and fixtures in each of the six rooms affected." Sierra grimaced. "The couch in the parlor has been damaged. It looks like the upholstery was ripped by a knife."

"Everyone pick a room to examine, preferably one you're

familiar with," Nick said. "I'll come by, and you can tell me what's been damaged."

The front hallway was little more than muddy. Although Kris hadn't begun setting anything up in his grand entry Christmas display, someone had removed the faux pine garland from the railings that framed the stairs to the second floor. The garland now lay in shredded bits of green, prickly plastic all over the tile.

Kaylee entered the study and gasped. Shredded ribbon covered the room in gray strips, and the other small touches she'd added had been smashed to the floor and ground into the slate-blue rug. Letting animals loose in the mansion was one thing—just a harmless prank. But this was intentionally malicious. The idea that someone had sabotaged the charitable work they'd tried to begin pricked at her heart. How could someone be so mean?

A knock sounded in the doorway, and she turned to see Reese Holt. An all-around good guy, he was the town's most sought after handyman and a couple of years older than Kaylee. Reese had been her grandmother's right-hand man for all things home repair, and now he sometimes did work around the cottage for Kaylee. He was one of the bright spots she'd encountered since moving to Orcas Island.

He stepped in and walked around the room, taking in the destruction, then met her gaze. She saw real concern in his blue eyes, and her heart skittered a bit.

"Hey, Reese," she said quietly.

"Hey to you too, stranger. How've you been?"

They hadn't seen each other around town lately. Kaylee had been busy at the flower shop, and Reese had been managing several contracting projects.

"Busy, to put it mildly." She gestured to the shells on the floor. "And now this."

"I heard about what happened with the designer and

everything that's been going on here at the mansion, and I wanted to see how you were holding up."

Kaylee nodded. "Thanks. We're literally picking up the pieces."

"I told Sierra I'd be glad to help repair any of the displays."

"Thank you. I know that will be a big help," Kaylee said. "Fortunately, I haven't brought any of the big stuff in. Not yet anyway."

"That's good to know. Only small things damaged?" Reese asked.

"I've lost only a few spools of ribbon and some knickknacks. All of that can easily be replaced."

"That's good. I just finished a kitchen remodel and a bathroom remodel, and that's it for bigger projects at the moment." Reese shrugged. "So if you need any help between now and the auction, you know where to find me."

"That I do." Kaylee watched him walk toward the door.

Reese paused in the doorway. "There's a new art show opening at Art Attack soon. Do you think you can take an evening off to visit the gallery and maybe have dinner?"

"Yes, I believe I can. In fact, I'd like that a lot." She grinned.

"Great. I'll find out the exact date for the opening and let you know so we can make plans—very soon." Reese smiled and left.

Yes, getting to know Reese had been one of the good parts about moving to Orcas Island, Kaylee reflected. She'd found herself slowing down since adopting island life. But she was also busy, learning to become her own boss and run her own business. She wanted to make her grandmother proud.

Kaylee supposed she ought to find a broom and a dustpan to sweep the carpet, the cushions of the wingback chairs, and the love seat. She reentered the grand hall, where Barbara and Duncan were looking through brooms and other cleaning supplies that were propped against the coat-tree.

"Any idea who could have done this?" Kaylee asked.

"Nope," Duncan said, grabbing a garbage bag. "I'll fess up to the animals. I thought it would be funny. I met a guy the other night who said he'd bring all the animals to start the design planning with a bang. I didn't count on the mud. But no way would I deliberately destroy another designer's work, and I definitely wouldn't damage my own."

Barbara snorted. "Right. I know the truth about you, Mr. McTavish. You've always had it in for Kris. He told me so. The Pacific Northwest wasn't big enough for the both of you to share, and now this lovely mansion and the youth of Orcas Island have been punished for it!"

Duncan rolled his eyes. "You're being a bit histrionic. But I know you've been through a lot in the past couple of days, so I don't blame you for being upset and lashing out."

"People know you threatened Kris. Did you forget to tell the police that?" Barbara snatched up a broom and a garbage bag. "If anyone comes looking for me, I'm headed to the dining room to clean up the mess that never should have happened."

Kaylee didn't miss the face Duncan made as Barbara stomped down the hallway. Nor did she miss the fresh tears in Barbara's eyes as she marched by.

"Just here for a broom," Kaylee said. "And a dustpan."

"Has anyone seen Meghan yet?" Duncan asked. "She hasn't shown up."

It was on the tip of Kaylee's tongue to say she'd seen her at the police station earlier, but she caught herself in time. There was no need to bring up speculation. Besides, she barely knew Duncan.

"I'm not sure if she knows what happened," Kaylee said. "Did anyone call her? Barbara called me."

"I don't know. Sierra called me," Duncan said.

Kaylee nodded, then returned to the study. As she cleaned up, she wondered where Meghan went after she left the sheriff's department. She knew it was worth noting that Kris's assistant hadn't shown up at the mansion. Of course, there could be a perfectly simple explanation.

Then she considered Barbara's insinuation that Duncan had had something to do with the vandalism and possibly even Kris's death. Maybe Duncan's lackadaisical attitude was a cover-up. People weren't always what they seemed, something she knew all too well from past experience.

"Your turn," Deputy Durham said as he walked into the room. "This is getting to be an unfortunate habit, us having unpleasant discussions in here."

"A lot has happened in two days." Kaylee paused her sweeping. "As far as I can tell, no furniture was damaged. Whoever threw things around and scattered shreds of ribbon all over the place didn't harm the upholstery or the carpet."

Nick surveyed the space. "Nothing seems to be different. We didn't take photos of this room for the investigation, but I was in here long enough to get the lay of the land, so to speak."

"I spent time in here yesterday morning to get the feel for the room and sketch a few ideas for my design," Kaylee said. "Today the ribbons were shredded, and some little things were broken up and strewn all over, but that's about it."

"All right. Let me know if you notice anything else. Thanks, Kaylee." Nick finished making notes and left the study.

Kaylee made quick work of sweeping. Now all that needed to be done to set the room right was a careful vacuuming of the old rug.

She needed to finish up here soon. While she had some regular local customers, she had extra orders for various Christmas events and parties on the island. It was getting to the point that she might need to hire a delivery driver to keep up with the orders so she could stay at the store to fill them. In January work would slow to a screeching halt while the locals and year-rounders hunkered down for the rest of the winter, but for now she had her hands full.

Kaylee headed home to pick up Bear, who probably thought she'd forgotten him for the day. They arrived at The Flower Patch after lunch, and she spent a good portion of the rest of her day receiving walk-in customers and trying to catch up on orders, with Mary's invaluable assistance.

Around three, Kaylee's cell phone chimed. She pulled it out to find a text from her grandmother: *Call me when you can.*

She'd been disappointed when her grandmother hadn't answered her call last evening. Kaylee had left her a message about what happened to Kris.

Kaylee decided to call her now before someone else stopped in at the shop. She missed her grandmother, and anytime she had the opportunity to talk to her was a plus in her book.

Her grandmother picked up after the second ring. "I got your message, and this is the first chance I've had to call you back."

Kaylee explained that they'd found Kris's body yesterday morning at the mansion and everything else that had happened, including the animal stampede and the vandalism discovered just that morning.

"I wonder what Kris's ties are to Orcas Island," Kaylee said. "Although he's been visiting regularly since the fall, which was when he and Barbara got together, I hadn't heard the name Carroll around before that."

"I don't know of any Carrolls either." Bea sighed. "Not for the first time do I wish your grandfather was around so I could ask him questions. He remembered everyone and everything that dealt with Orcas. I imagine he might have known of Kristopher

Carroll too. A name like that would stand out. Kris Carroll—almost a play on 'Christmas carol.'"

"I wish Grandpa was here too," Kaylee said. "I did hear someone mention that Kris might have lived in Turtle Cove when he was in his twenties."

"Then perhaps he came to visit a relative for the summer, like some kids did. He could have been one of the boys who'd work the fishing boats. They always needed help, and when boys were old enough, they'd sign on to work for the summer during high school and sometimes college."

"That sounds like a good possibility."

"Do they know how he died yet?" Bea asked.

"They're not sure, but they believe he likely died elsewhere and his body was moved to the mansion."

"How terrible."

"I can't stop thinking about who might have wanted to hurt him," Kaylee admitted. "Nick Durham asked for my help with the plant and soil forensics. It'll feel good to be back in the lab again, even for a short time." At that statement, she heard her own voice brightening.

"You're not regretting that you bought the shop, are you?"

"Oh no, not for a minute. I love the shop and the Petal Pushers and Orcas Island. And helping the sheriff's department helps me dabble in botany and keep up my skills. It feels good to know I'm needed."

"That's wonderful to hear. I know I left my shop in good hands with you. Anyway, I'm glad you called. I have a book club meeting with some friends this afternoon, so I need to go. Talk again soon?"

"Definitely. Love you."

"Love you too, dear."

Smiling, Kaylee set down her phone. Her grandmother was

but a call away.

She almost regretted her words about the lab. But it was true. Floral design exercised her artistic side. But the plant taxonomy satisfied her scientific side and was something that had fascinated her from childhood.

She looked forward to seeing what, if anything, her analysis would tell her about Kristopher Carroll's last moments.

5

The next morning Kaylee received a call from island coroner Giles Akin, asking if she could stop by the funeral home. He'd collected samples, and that afternoon his preparation room would be free for her to examine what he'd collected.

She left Bear at the shop with Mary after giving him a treat and the promise of a nice walk that evening weather permitting.

Soon Kaylee stepped into Akin Funeral Chapel. It smelled like lavender, as if someone were diffusing essential oils. The fragrance was soothing.

Giles met her at the door and shook her hand. "Thanks for coming. I know the police are grateful for your help."

"I'm glad to do it." Kaylee followed him down a hall lined with framed photos.

They entered the room at the end of the hall, and Giles pointed to a long metal table situated against the wall. A stack of vials made a neat line beside a pile of small plastic bags. All the samples bore white labels, and she could make out lettering on each. Someone had also set out a legal pad and a pen beside a microscope.

She stepped over to the vials. "Do you have plans to send his body to Seattle?"

"No, I don't have an inclination at this time," Giles answered. "I'm confident that between the two of us we can accomplish things here almost as quickly. I'll only send the remains if necessary."

"I'm glad you have that confidence, so thank you," Kaylee said. "Has a service been scheduled for Mr. Carroll yet?"

Giles shook his head. "According to his financial manager in Seattle, he had no family. At least none that are willing or able to step up to make arrangements. His receptionist is beyond distraught and didn't know anything about his final plans. Although Mr. Carroll had the means to make prearrangements upon the occasion of his passing, it seems he did not."

It was sad that no one had made any plans for Mr. Carroll. Kaylee couldn't imagine being without any family to make arrangements for her if needed.

Giles moved as if to leave the room, then paused. "Someone local has stepped up, though, asking about arrangements and offering a solution. Ms. Sierra Underwood inquired about the cost for having a simple memorial for Mr. Carroll and if I would accept payment for seeing to his body. Of course, that type of memorial must be put off because we are unable to release the body at this point. However, anyone who wishes to can hold a service without a body."

Kaylee found Sierra's offer touching. Maybe there was something she could do to help. She imagined the Petal Pushers would want to pitch in as well.

"I'll leave you to your work." Giles headed off to his own office, leaving her in the silent room.

Kaylee tried not to think of where she presently sat as an embalming room but as a lab for her to get work done and find some answers as to what might have happened to Kris Carroll.

She called the sheriff's department and left a message for Nick, telling him she was at the funeral chapel and preparing to examine the samples collected by Giles.

The first set of vials contained soil samples, with labels on the vials indicating where the samples were taken from, such as the soles of Kris's boots, under his fingernails, and the hem of his blue jeans.

The next set of collections had labels like *beard, hair, shirt, fingernails, ears,* and *mouth.*

"I've already sent blood, saliva, and tissue samples to the forensic examiner's lab in Seattle and asked for an expedited report." Giles's voice echoed off the tile walls behind her.

Kaylee jumped.

"Sorry. I didn't mean to startle you. I just remembered and came back to tell you."

"That's all right. I haven't really gotten started yet." Kaylee pulled a pair of latex gloves from a nearby cardboard box and slipped them on.

"I'm not sure how much you'll find, but I know the sheriff is glad to have you here in the area. We couldn't do this if you weren't here. You're going to save us some valuable time. No telling how long we'd have to wait if we shipped everything off. Not that I mind their help on the mainland, but sometimes doing things yourself gets them accomplished faster."

"Thanks. I hope I can find some answers here."

"I'll let you get to it, then." Again, Giles walked out and closed the door behind him.

Kaylee turned back to the microscope, took the first vial of soil samples, and made a slide to examine.

She peered through the viewfinder, pulling the images into focus. Soil, typical for Orcas Island. Where was this sample taken? She glanced at the label: *soles of boots.*

If Kris had walked into the mansion of his own accord, any soil could come from outside and would match. If the last place he'd walked was somewhere else, well, there would be a strong likelihood that the sample wouldn't match.

She needed to get samples from the mansion's grounds, particularly the parking area, if there were any that had been collected. Maybe the sheriff's office crime scene processors had gathered samples already. She'd have to ask Nick.

Another question popped into her mind. How did Kris

arrive at the mansion the night of the reception? He had a car he'd driven around the island, but she couldn't recall if it had been at the mansion when his body had been found. Or maybe the car was parked somewhere else, like wherever he'd been staying. She would ask Nick about that too.

Kaylee studied the rest of the samples one by one. She found some dried grass and a few partially decomposed leaves but nothing notable as far as any traces of vegetation went.

In the sample from under Kris's fingernails, she discovered flecks of greenery no bigger than a pinpoint.

Was that a tiny bit of hair? It was so small, but it definitely looked like a human hair under the microscope. She labeled the slide *fingernails* to correspond with the vial and set it aside for her report.

Kaylee supposed finding little, if any, vegetation was a good thing. Otherwise pollen and flora of all types might be part of the samples, and she would have to try to sort through it all. Then again, the absence of plant evidence could also be a bad thing. Without a trace of vegetation, it would be hard to tell exactly where Kris had been during his final moments.

Kaylee prepared another slide and placed it under the microscope to study. A few hard-to-see fibers caught her eye. They didn't look like vegetation. They appeared dark blue and woven.

She magnified the threads. Now they looked royal blue. Where had they come from? The mansion? But there was no carpet in the grand entryway, and the carpet in the study was a dusky blue, more of a slate color, not like the color of these threads.

Kaylee picked up the pen and wrote notes about the vial and what the contents had revealed under extreme magnification.

The more she examined each sample, the more questions rose. The same kind of questions the sheriff's office would likely ask too. They'd need answers. Or maybe they already had some possible answers, and the information she now gathered would help confirm what they suspected.

The minutes ticked away, and Kaylee finally noticed the crick in her neck. She stood and stretched, muscles aching. How long had she been here?

Kaylee glanced at her phone. She'd worked steadily for more than two hours—and she was supposed to meet the delivery truck at the ferry in fifteen minutes!

While Orcas Island had pretty much everything anyone could need, fresh flowers had to arrive by ferry from Seattle. She didn't want to ask Mary to go because she was holding down the shop while Kaylee was here at the funeral chapel.

She noted where she stopped looking at samples, then set them back exactly the way she'd found them.

Kaylee called the sheriff's department, and Aida was able to put her directly through to Nick.

"Have you been busy?" the deputy asked.

"As a matter of fact, I'm wrapping up for now over at Akin's. Can you please let the sheriff know that I'll have a report of my findings ready for him by this evening?"

"Sure thing."

"I would have it finished sooner, but I need to meet the ferry in fifteen minutes."

"I understand you have other things to tend to. We're still working through evidence and the information from the interviews too."

The call ended, and Kaylee continued cleaning up. Fortunately, the microscope enabled her to take a screenshot of the sample images, and she loaded those onto a thumb drive so she could look at them later while typing her report for the police. She would give them a copy of the images as well.

Within a few minutes, she was zipping along the road back to

Turtle Cove and to the harbor ferry landing. The day had turned out clear, with just a bit of a nip in the wind. Kaylee inhaled deeply. She never tired of the scent of the sea air that swept in from Puget Sound.

Whenever stresses came, even in a beautiful place like Orcas Island, Kaylee needed only a few moments like this to let the surroundings calm her.

She pulled up at the ferry landing right on time to meet the delivery truck at the edge of the parking lot.

On the delivery schedule today were more poinsettias—the most popular flower this time of year—red roses, holly, and carnations, which she always kept on hand for Aida. She wouldn't order the fresh pine garland for her display at the mansion until just prior to the final setup of the room.

Kris's floral order was scheduled to arrive next week, which she reminded herself might need to be changed depending on what happened with the open house and his design.

As Kaylee signed for the flowers on a clipboard, a car passed them by. She recognized the driver from Northern Lights Inn, the most popular local accommodations.

A young woman hopped out of the vehicle and marched up to the ticket booth for the ferry.

It was Meghan Benson.

Meghan glanced around, and a sheepish look crossed her face when her eyes locked with Kaylee's. She waved, then scurried onto the boarding bridge for the ferry.

Hadn't Deputy Garcia told Meghan not to leave town without telling the police? Of course, Kaylee would have no way to know, but something in Meghan's expression told her Kris's assistant was slipping away without an okay from the sheriff's department.

That wasn't good. But maybe Meghan had some business affairs to tend to for Kris. Even though he'd passed away, it didn't mean everything would stop. Although, Kaylee mused, much business could be conducted via phone and computer.

The ferry's horn blared, signaling the departure to the mainland within ten minutes.

"Until next week?" the flower delivery driver asked as he took the clipboard from Kaylee.

"Until next week." She returned to her own vehicle, then headed back to The Flower Patch.

No sooner had she unloaded the floral shipment and given Bear a bone than the bell chimed over the door and in walked a customer.

Bear stopped chewing his bone to woof.

Smiling, Kaylee greeted the brunette who looked to be about her age. The woman appeared a bit frantic, and Kaylee steeled herself for a potential floral catastrophe.

The woman introduced herself as Janice Humphreys. "I ordered some flower arrangements for my daughter's sweet sixteen birthday party."

Kaylee consulted her calendar. "Yes, I remember. I have it on the schedule. Do you need to add anything to your order or change it?"

"There's been a date change. I placed the order for the twentieth, but we need to move it up to the eighteenth." Mrs. Humphreys sighed. "My mother-in-law has to take an earlier flight home, and she doesn't want to get on the early ferry to the airport."

"I understand completely." Kaylee reached for her paper desk calendar. She'd make her own adjustments for this order. She had a wedding party and church decorations due the same day, but she'd figure it out. "Is the party still at six?"

"Yes, the time hasn't changed. Just the date. The restaurant said you can come at five to set up in the party room."

"That'll work for me," Kaylee said. "No problem at all."

Mrs. Humphreys stepped closer to the counter. "I think it's awful about that nice man Mr. Carroll. We've already bought tickets to the House of Christmas Trees, and we sure hope it's going to be successful."

"We're hoping so too."

"They're not canceling, are they?" Mrs. Humphreys asked.

"No, I'm on the planning committee, and there aren't any plans to cancel."

"That's good news. But I was alarmed to hear the latest news reports that said Mr. Carroll had been shot. Why would anyone do such a thing to him? I wonder if the police have found any leads." Mrs. Humphreys shook her head and frowned. "This island has always felt like a safe place, but now I'm worried."

"I really don't know why anyone would want to harm him," Kaylee admitted. "I'm still rather new in town, but I don't feel unsafe. I know the sheriff and his deputies are doing all they can to find out exactly what happened."

Mrs. Humphreys stayed to chat a bit more about the holidays, life with a teenager, and how much shopping she still had to do for the sweet sixteen party and Christmas, then whirled out the door.

Kaylee's head spun after the woman left. But she reminded herself that part of the charm of The Flower Patch—besides it being in a Victorian mansion—was its connection to the community and the island, all thanks to her grandmother. Over the years her grandmother had worked hard to build relationships with her customers, and Kaylee would do her best to maintain and grow them.

She looked down at Bear who was still chewing his bone. "This is part of the job, right?"

The dog barked in response, then returned to his treat.

Kaylee laughed and got back to work. As she sorted the newest blooms and put them into the refrigerator case, the front door chimed again.

Jessica blew into the store, looking almost as frantic as Mrs. Humphreys. She wore her Death by Chocolate apron, her hair pulled back with some strands escaping, as if they too were panicking. "Oh, Kaylee!"

"What is it?" Kaylee rushed over to her friend.

Jessica took a deep breath. "I found a gun in the Dumpster behind my store."

6

Kaylee gasped. "A gun?"

Jessica nodded. "I was taking out the trash this morning after the breakfast rush and saw something. I pulled it out, and there was a handgun. I called the police, and Deputy Garcia came right over and took the gun with her."

"I can't believe it," Kaylee said. "How long do you think the gun was there?"

Jessica paced the floor. "I don't know. The trash service empties the bin once a week, so it's been there less than a week. I'm surprised I hadn't noticed it before."

"I wonder if the gun being stashed there had anything to do with Kris Carroll now that the news is out."

Jessica stopped pacing. "What news?"

If Mrs. Humphreys knew about the gunshot, then surely Kaylee could say something to Jessica. "Well, Kris was shot—"

"Shot?" Jessica exclaimed.

"That's what Nick told me, but he's not sure if it happened before or after he was dead. Which makes no sense. Unless someone was trying to make sure he was dead." Kaylee shook her head. "It's the weirdest thing."

"So, did you find anything with those samples?"

"It's too early to say," Kaylee answered. "All I can do is give the sheriff my report on the evidence, but I have no idea what that will tell them or even who it'll point to, if anyone."

Jessica walked over to Bear and scratched behind his ears. "How's the House of Christmas Trees going?"

"I haven't heard anything since our meeting the other day."

Kaylee sat down on a stool behind the counter. "Sierra was leaning toward postponing it, so she was going to check on the scheduling with the mansion owner. Since there are no arrangements planned for Kris at the moment, I think we should continue on like we are right now, selling tickets and promoting."

"You look like you know something else. Tell me." Jessica joined her at the counter and sat down on the stool next to her.

"I saw Meghan Benson getting a ride to the ferry when I was picking up my delivery at the harbor."

Jessica jumped up. "She's not leaving for good, is she?"

"I don't know. She was told not to leave town. Maybe she had to take care of something back at the office, something that Kris normally would have done—"

The front door to the shop opened, its bell jingling.

Bear barked, and both Kaylee and Jessica glanced at the door.

Sierra walked in. She had dark circles under her eyes, but it didn't look like she'd been crying. "I'm glad I caught you here. We're in the clear to go forward with the original date for the event. The more I considered it, the more I believe it's the best thing for us to do, given the circumstances."

"I think you made the right decision," Kaylee said.

"Plus, all the posters and tickets are already dated," Sierra added, "and if we delayed the event by a week, it would be too close to Christmas."

"What if we dedicate the event to Mr. Carroll? Maybe there's a way we can memorialize him and include it as part of his design," Kaylee suggested. "It would be nice if we put his picture beside his display, either on an easel or something like that."

Sierra nodded and brushed tears from her eyes. "That's a really great idea."

"What's wrong, Sierra?" Jessica took a step closer to the young woman and touched her arm. "I think it's more than just everything that's gone wrong with the open house already. Am I right?"

Sierra nodded. "Christmas isn't the same this year without Mom. It won't ever be the same. I'm trying to make it through the holidays, but it's tough."

"I'm so sorry." Kaylee retrieved a box of tissues from behind the counter and offered it to Sierra.

"Thank you." Sierra took a tissue and wiped her eyes with it. "For years, it was always just the two of us for the holidays. Now Mom's gone. I tried to get through this first year without her by working hard on the House of Christmas Trees. I've also enjoyed being around all of you. But it's still been difficult."

"If you need to step down from the committee," Kaylee said softly, "I'm sure we can get someone else to do it. The bulk of the planning is done, and the only thing left is the execution."

"No, I won't do that. Then Barbara will step in and take over everything and do whatever she wants." Sierra waved her hands. "But enough about that woman's pushiness. We're going forward as planned, no matter what."

"We'll get it all done on time," Kaylee reassured her. "And we'll make sure Kris's design meets everyone's high expectations."

"I know. It's going to be great," Sierra said.

"Mr. Akin told me that you inquired about holding a simple memorial for Mr. Carroll," Kaylee said to Sierra.

"I was only thinking out loud when I talked to Mr. Akin about it," Sierra admitted. "I don't have the money for arrangements, and right now isn't the best time to ask anyone else to chip in. I'm sorry he made it sound as if I was serious about planning something."

"I wonder if Kris Carroll even had a will," Jessica remarked. "I have one. I want to make sure my daughter is taken care of even though she's an adult, and I want to have a say in what happens to my things."

"That's smart of you," Sierra said. "A lot of people don't have wills. I'm not sure if Kris did."

"A will could tell us a great deal about who would benefit from Kris's passing." Kaylee lowered her voice. "And maybe who might want him dead."

After a busy afternoon at the shop, Kaylee and Bear returned home. She recalled her promise to Bear to take a walk, so she put on his newest sweater and snapped his leash to his collar. Then they headed out the front door of Wildflower Cottage.

Just as they did so, a familiar truck pulled into the driveway.

Reese parked behind her Escape and got out, a grin on his face. "Hey there."

Bear yipped and strained at his leash, so Kaylee let go of it. The dog ran to Reese, who bent down to pet him.

"Hey there yourself." She couldn't help but smile as she joined them. "What brings you by?"

Reese straightened, then smiled as Bear danced around his feet. "I found out when the new show opens at Art Attack, and I was hoping you were still interested in going with me."

"Of course. When is it?"

"Friday night. I thought we could go to dinner, then catch the show. It's the last one of the year, and it's supposed to be really good. Sam Miller is from Eastsound, and he paints landscapes of the Pacific Northwest. His show includes paintings from all over the San Juan Islands. I understand a few are of places right here in Turtle Cove."

Kaylee was immediately intrigued. But she thought of her busy weekend ahead. "What time were you planning to go? I have a full workday on Saturday, starting with deliveries in the morning, and I'll be at the mansion after that. So I don't want to be out too late."

"I can pick you up around six. The gallery opens at seven and the show is open until nine thirty, so if we eat first, we'll have plenty of time to check out the gallery. Your pick of restaurant."

Kaylee hesitated as butterflies battled each other in her stomach. "How does O'Brien's by the harbor sound? I love their fish and chips."

Reese nodded. "That's good for me. They make a mean burger. I'll see you Friday." He gave Bear another pat, then sauntered back to his truck and waved at her as he headed down the driveway.

Kaylee smiled to herself. Was this really a date? Sort of? She knew the food would be great, the company excellent, and she'd been meaning to go to one of Art Attack's art openings. She'd always heard great things about them.

Orcas Island wasn't a big city, but the gallery was part of the culture of Turtle Cove. It hosted all kinds of art shows, featuring local Native American art, along with paintings, sculpture, and pottery. More often than not, a local musician would provide live entertainment, usually on guitar or saxophone. It was owned by a talented painter named Nora Keller.

"What do you think, Bear?" she asked as they walked along the driveway.

He stopped and sat on his haunches as if thinking carefully. Then he looked up at her and gave her a doggy smile.

"So, you think I should just relax and enjoy myself and stop thinking so much?"

He wagged his tail.

Instead of walking nearby, Kaylee decided to drive back to town and spend some time at the dog park. Bear would love that.

She strapped him into his doggy seat belt in the Escape, then got in and headed for the park.

Despite her words to Bear—and to herself—she continued to contemplate as they drove to town. Christmas would be different this year compared to other years. She'd found herself starting over in a place that was close to her heart—Turtle Cove. But in the past, Turtle Cove had had her grandparents in it.

She missed her grandfather with a heartache that persisted in spite of the years since his passing, and although her grandmother was very much alive and loving her new life in Arizona, Kaylee realized she missed her with almost as deep an ache. Wildflower Cottage and The Flower Patch still had her grandmother's fingerprints all over them, both literally and figuratively. In every room, Kaylee half-expected her grandmother to walk around the next corner.

She sighed. Christmas definitely wouldn't be the same without them this year.

Downtown Turtle Cove twinkled, already decked out for Christmas. The mud from a few days ago would soon be covered up by a fresh snowfall, the weather report assured them. She parked in the closest spot to the dog park, and Bear turned and pressed his nose against the window. When Kaylee opened the door, unbuckled his seat belt, and snapped on his leash, Bear bounded out and rushed ahead, his short legs pumping.

After frolicking with a few new canine friends for a while, Bear looked up at her, panting.

"I think you've had enough excitement for one day, Bear Dog. Let's go." They returned to the Escape and set off.

On a whim, she motored down Main Street and passed The Flower Patch. Even when it was closed, the grand Victorian house looked welcoming. Next door, lights still glowed at Death by Chocolate. And across the street, DeeDee was locking up Between the Lines for the evening.

Kaylee stopped at the curb in front of the bookstore and rolled down her window.

"Hey, Kaylee!" DeeDee called out. "What brings you back here?"

"Bear and I stopped at the dog park." She glanced over at her furry friend and smiled.

"Long day?" DeeDee asked.

"Yes, but a good one."

"I always forget how busy the days leading up to Christmas get," DeeDee said. "Polly and Zoe have their holiday choir concert tonight at school, so I'm off to get supper out of the slow cooker and on the table before we head over to the school. I can't have my daughters passing out from hunger onstage, can I?"

Kaylee laughed.

"Hey, ladies!" Jessica hung out the door of Death by Chocolate. "You two going to stay out here in the chilly air and talk until dark, or would you like to come in for a hot cup of coffee?"

"I'm on my way home. The girls have a choir concert tonight," DeeDee explained. "I'll take a rain check on that coffee, though."

"Tell Polly and Zoe I know they'll do great," Jessica said.

"I will. See you both tomorrow." DeeDee waved as she walked toward her car.

"How about you, Kaylee?" Jessica asked. "Care to come inside?"

"Sure. I've got Bear with me. Is that okay?"

"Of course. I'm closing up anyway."

Kaylee turned off the ignition, unbuckled Bear from his seat belt, and climbed from the vehicle. Bear hopped out behind her.

When they reached the shop, Bear hesitated at the threshold as delightful smells streamed past him. He looked up at Kaylee, giving her a questioning look, as if he sought permission to go inside.

"It's okay, Bear. This time we can both go in." Kaylee tugged on his leash, and he walked in beside her. "Bear wasn't so sure this is allowed."

Jessica crouched down and fondled his floppy ears. "It's quite all right. And if your mommy allows, I have some leftover pound cake for you."

"It's not chocolate, is it?"

"Absolutely not." Bear had flopped onto his side, so Jessica rubbed his belly. "I would never put this little guy in danger."

Kaylee grinned at Bear's ability to melt any heart. "Well, okay, he can have a bite of cake. But just this once."

Bear stood, his tail whipping from side to side and his nose twitching.

Jessica headed into the kitchen and prep area, then emerged with a thick slice of pound cake on a paper plate. She set it on the floor.

Bear sniffed the cake, then gobbled it up in a few bites. He carefully cleaned the plate, then sniffed the floor around it for any leftover crumbs that might have escaped.

Kaylee chuckled. "I feel the same way about your chocolate cake. I think I've gained a little weight since moving here. Hence my walk tonight."

"Hmm." Jessica's eyes sparkled. "I was going to offer you some truffles to go with this cup of coffee, but if you don't want them I'll just put them back."

"I think I've earned them. At least this way I'll break even on the calories."

Smiling, Jessica poured a fresh cup of home brew and slid a trio of truffles topped with chocolate espresso powder in Kaylee's direction.

Kaylee took a long sip of the hot coffee. "That's really good." She nibbled on one of the truffles and glanced at Oliver on the counter. His leaves still appeared a bit droopy. "Is something still not right in Oliver's world?"

"I don't know." Jessica touched one of the geranium's leaves. "Maybe he's recovering from the shock of Kris Carroll passing away. Or maybe there's something else on the horizon. Something bad for another resident of Turtle Cove." Her voice held an unmistakably ominous tone.

Kaylee stopped and stared at her, not sure how to respond.

Jessica burst into laughter. "I'm kidding. Sort of. Tell me something good that happened today. Sometimes the way people behave, especially customers, leaves me with little hope in human nature."

Kaylee thought for a moment. "Well, Reese asked me to dinner, and then we're going to the opening at Art Attack Friday night."

"Good for you. I'm glad you're finally getting out for something besides work and the Petal Pushers meetings. We're thrilled to have you, of course," Jessica added, "but there's more to life than the shop and our club."

"I still feel like I'm getting to know the town—even though I can't count the number of visits I made when I was a kid—and learning how to run the flower shop," Kaylee admitted.

"You're doing a fabulous job." Jessica patted her hand. "So do you have any exciting plans for Christmas?"

Kaylee's mood fell despite the fact that a delicious truffle had just melted in her mouth. "I haven't figured out what to do yet. My parents are in Florida with my brother and his family, and Grandma is in Arizona. The holidays are going to feel very different this year. I'm not a child anymore. I'm used to Christmas the way I celebrate it. But for me, Orcas Island was Orcas Island because Grandma was here."

Jessica nodded. "When Mila went off to college, I thought I'd about explode with missing her. Everything around here was the same, but it was like there was a big hole where she used to be. I've got my house, my shop, my whole routine. But without her, nothing felt the same."

Kaylee took another sip of her coffee. "Change is a part of life, they say."

"Goodness knows you've seen many changes in the past year. A job loss, a career change, and a major move." Jessica looked thoughtful. "You just go on and enjoy a night out with Reese. And you never know what might happen at Christmastime."

"Hopefully it won't involve finding another body."

Bear barked as if in agreement.

7

True to his word, Reese arrived at Wildflower Cottage on Friday right before six. He parked his truck behind her Escape, and Kaylee watched him approach from the front window.

Reese looked like he was ready to go out on the town. Gone was his customary Dodgers baseball cap, and his hair was carefully styled but not too fussy. He wore a button-down shirt and khakis instead of his usual plaid flannel and worn jeans.

Oh my. Kaylee swallowed hard.

She glanced down at her own outfit: a sensible purple sweater that brought out her green eyes, jeans, and insulated boots. Suddenly she felt underdressed. It was hardly a date-night ensemble. But this was not a romantic date, she reminded herself. It was simply a night out to relax with a relatively new friend and a chance to perhaps meet some people in town. A chance to get to know more of Turtle Cove without her grandmother in it. The other year-rounders in town had businesses, some seasonal, but the Art Attack gallery seemed to be a popular spot no matter what the season.

Her doorbell rang, and Bear beat Kaylee to the door. When she opened it, Bear rushed in little circles around Reese, yipping. He stopped and put his front paws against Reese's leg. The man grinned and reached down to scratch behind the dog's ears.

Kaylee smiled at Reese. "I'm ready, and I have my appetite too."

He laughed, a warm, rich sound to her ears. "Great. Because I've reserved a table by the window for us at O'Brien's."

A dinner reservation? Kaylee stifled a sigh. This was sounding less and less like a casual night out with each minute that passed. If he was serious about a table by the window, they'd be on display in front of most of Turtle Cove. But somehow she didn't think O'Brien's was the kind of place that took reservations. She hoped he was just teasing.

"Are you ready?" Reese asked.

Kaylee nodded and put on her coat and scarf, then said good-bye to Bear.

The dog gave her a pitiful look as if to say, "Go on without me and have your fun. I'll be fine here. You know, alone. Forever." Then he slithered toward his bed while Reese and Kaylee laughed at his drama.

As soon as they walked out the door, Kaylee felt the chill of a promised dusting of snow hanging in the air. She pulled her coat tighter.

Reese opened the truck's passenger door with a flourish. "Ma'am." The cab was warm inside, the engine still running.

"Why, thank you." Kaylee's cheeks blazed as he shut the door for her. What was she thinking? *Relax*, she told herself. *This is not a date. Reese is just polite.*

They headed into town and toward the waterfront, where several businesses overlooked the harbor. One of those was O'Brien's. Kaylee had discovered the place one night when she'd been out exploring on her own not too long after moving to Turtle Cove. To her delight, they had a dog-friendly patio where she'd had dinner several times with Bear.

"You're awfully quiet," Reese said.

"It's been a long week with a lot going on. I finished my report for Sheriff Maddox and landed two more last-minute wedding gigs before New Year's." She shook her head. "What is it with people getting married in December, anyway? I mean, the holidays can be busy enough without adding a wedding to the mix."

"I couldn't tell you the answer to that one. I prefer to keep things simple." He fell silent and flipped the switch for the turn signal, then pulled into the parking lot.

"I completely understand," she said. "Why get bogged down in the details for an event that will only last a few hours? Of course a wedding is a significant event and should be memorable, but just in my few months here, I've seen brides complicate things for themselves to no end."

Kaylee closed her eyes. *Oops.* She'd heard that Reese had been jilted by a fiancée. Was it Jessica who'd told her that? She hoped the mention of wedding planning didn't bother him. Anyway, it didn't seem like it was too much of a sore spot for him anymore, but it probably made him a bit hesitant to head toward the altar again. That was actually reassuring. Surely he didn't see this as a romantic date.

Reese parked and killed the engine. "I like how you think." He shot her a grin in the dark, then left the truck and circled around to her side. When he opened the door, the sound of jazz poured into the truck's cab.

"Thanks," Kaylee said simply as she hopped out. She didn't want to continue the conversation about weddings. The romance department hadn't been very good to her either, and while she didn't steer away from it, she was in no hurry to approach the altar herself.

They crossed the parking lot and headed for the restaurant made of old barn wood, which resembled a stretched-out fisherman's shack. There was a deck on all four sides, part of which extended over the water.

"I'm glad you picked one of my favorite spots in town." Reese opened the restaurant door and scanned the dining room. "Looks like we'll get in pretty quickly too."

No one waited in the foyer to be seated, though the restaurant's driftwood-style tables were mostly occupied.

"Great timing," Kaylee said over the sound of music pouring out of the speakers in the ceiling. The peppy tune made her want to do a little jig, but she figured that wouldn't be the best idea at the moment. *See? No reservation and I am enjoying myself.*

As the hostess escorted Kaylee and Reese to an open table, Kaylee couldn't help looking around at all the oceanic paraphernalia that lined the walls and even hung in netting stretched across the ceiling. There were starfish, anchors, fish of all kinds, paintings of ships on the high seas, and old-fashioned lanterns. There was even a framed sailor's outfit hanging on the far wall. She always felt like she noticed something new on each visit. *Like that octopus in the corner.*

The hostess stopped at a table in the front window overlooking the parking lot. "Here you go. I'm sorry it's not a harbor view, although there's not much to see out there in the dark." The hostess squinted across the dining room. "Hold on a sec. A table just got cleared over there. Please follow me." She led them to the harbor side of the restaurant.

"I almost thought you were serious when you said you'd reserved a table by the window," Kaylee said over her shoulder to Reese as he pulled out her chair.

"Hey, what can I say? It's all about location, right?" He grinned as they took their seats.

Thirty minutes later, as they talked over their food, Reese's face took on a more serious expression. "So, how are things at Wildflower Cottage and The Flower Patch? I have to admit I'd gotten used to Bea calling me to fix this or that. You sure there's nothing you need help with?"

"Thanks for the offer, but there's nothing that needs fixing at the moment. I think Grandma had you do all the work before I arrived. No leaks, no projects." Kaylee picked up a thick French fry and dipped it into the restaurant's house ketchup seasoning. Whatever the place did to ketchup she didn't know, but they should keep on doing it.

"Well, then, how's the House of Christmas Trees coming along?" Reese took a bite of his burger.

Kaylee shrugged. "There's not much to tell right now. Tickets are selling, and the committee is going forward with the promotion, in spite of everything that's happened. We all pretty much agreed—especially Barbara—that Kris would have wanted us to go on."

"Good. But who's going to pick up the slack for Kris's design? Can Meghan do it herself?"

"I'm going to help her. She made a trip to Kris's office in Seattle earlier in the week to take care of some things." She had finally followed her conscience and texted Nick to ask about Meghan's apparent escape, and he'd assured her that Meghan had cleared it with him before she left. "But it always helps to have an extra pair of hands."

"If you'd like, I don't mind being your extra pair of hands. Really. I can trim stems or poke things into florist foam, whatever you need me to do."

Kaylee was touched. "That's a very generous offer. Thank you."

"It's my pleasure," Reese said. "I've seen Bea work her floral magic I don't know how many times over the years. You just tell me what to do, and Mary can run the shop. I'm not sure you'd want to close for an entire day of setup."

"You're right—I wouldn't." Kaylee smiled at Reese's enthusiasm. "And it's very true. Mary's a huge help at the shop, and I'm quite busy with two more weddings and a sweet sixteen party. So you're hired. We're going to set up at the mansion on Thursday. The open house officially goes from Friday evening through Sunday afternoon. The auction takes place Friday night, and the displays will stay set up for the weekend. Then after Sunday, we get to take it all down so the auction winners can take their decorations home."

"Whew." He wiped imaginary sweat from his forehead. "That sounds like a lot. But I'm up for it."

"You sure you won't be too busy?" Kaylee asked.

"No. Things have really slowed down. I've finished all my remodels, and people aren't planning any big projects during the holidays. Nobody needs help with outdoor work at the moment. My schedule is almost wide open unless there's an emergency. Of course I'm meeting up with people to book projects that will start after New Year's, so that's about it for now."

"It sounds like a plan. I'm going to prep all the plants and flowers on Thursday morning, so I'll need you at the shop early. Then we'll load up my vehicle and your truck and head to the mansion." She smiled at Reese. "I'm sorry if I sound reluctant to ask for help. I'm used to taking care of things myself."

"I understand. But I like that about you." He gave her a long look.

Kaylee gazed out the window, hoping the heat in her face and neck wasn't manifesting as unsightly red splotches. This was feeling like a date again. Although she was definitely relieved to have an extra pair of hands to count on for the House of Christmas Trees.

Judging by the number of vehicles parked on the street, in the parking lot, and along the side streets, Art Attack was the hottest place in Turtle Cove that evening. Reese had to circle the block three times to find a parking spot.

As soon as they entered the art gallery, Kaylee felt the warmth of the crowd drawing them in.

Owner Nora Keller greeted them enthusiastically. "I'm so glad you both made it." The painter wore a peasant blouse over a broomstick skirt, and her long blonde hair hung down one shoulder in a single braid.

"Glad to be here," Kaylee said. She took a moment to glance around the space. Nora's husband, Christian, played smooth jazz on his saxophone as a soothing background to the murmur of the crowd—the perfect accompaniment for viewing the most recent works of Orcas Island artist Sam Miller. She spotted a few of her flower shop customers and Sheriff Eddie Maddox, along with his wife, Susan.

"What do you think of Sam Miller's paintings of Orcas Island in the winter?" Nora asked.

"They're amazing," Reese replied, awe in his voice.

Kaylee silently agreed with Reese's assessment as she surveyed the framed watercolors, which showed various landmarks around the island, including the mansion and the historic lighthouse. She and the Petal Pushers held their meetings in the keeper's quarters at the Old Cape Lighthouse located near the flower shop. Then her gaze landed on a beautiful depiction of a building that was as familiar to her as her own name.

"The Flower Patch!" she exclaimed. Her heart swelled to see such a lovely interpretation of her grandmother's shop.

She checked the painting's price tag, but it was a little too steep for her budget. She turned to Nora. "Does Mr. Miller sell prints of this painting? If he does, I'd love to buy two." She knew a print would be a special gift for her grandmother, and the other one would look wonderful behind the register inside the shop.

"I'm not sure," Nora said. "You can ask Sam yourself, and if he does have a print, I'd be happy to frame it for you." She nudged Kaylee's arm. "Come on. I'll introduce you."

Nora ushered Kaylee and Reese over to Sam Miller.

The artist of the evening had gray hair and an equally gray handlebar mustache. He turned his attention to them. "Good evening. Great party as always, Nora."

"Thank you. Sam, I'd like you to meet Reese Holt and Kaylee Bleu. Reese has a carpentry business here in Turtle Cove. Kaylee owns The Flower Patch, the old Victorian house that is featured in one of your paintings."

Reese and Sam shook hands. "It's nice to meet you," Reese said.

"And you, Reese." Sam turned his attention to Kaylee. "Ms. Bleu, it's a pleasure. So that's your flower shop. How wonderful to have a business that brings so much joy to so many." Sam extended his weathered hand, and Kaylee took it. As they shook hands, his blue eyes twinkled at her and he inclined his head slightly.

Kaylee couldn't help but smile at his courtly manner. "Thank you. It's nice to meet you. Please call me Kaylee. Beatrice Lyons is my grandmother, and I bought The Flower Patch from her last summer. I'm not sure if you know her."

"Ah yes, I'm well acquainted with Bea, and I also knew your late grandfather. It was a treat for me to paint the old Victorian mansion." Sam scanned the gallery wall where the paintings hung. "A treasure of Orcas Island, as are all its older structures."

"I've become an instant fan of your work tonight," Kaylee said. "I'm curious if you sell prints of your paintings."

"I'm afraid I don't at the moment. I'm searching for a new printer. The one I worked with closed. I'm guessing you're interested in a print of The Flower Patch?"

"Yes, I'd love to purchase two of them."

Sam twirled his mustache. "Nora, please put a sold sign on that painting."

"Mr. Miller, I'm afraid I can't—" Kaylee began.

"Nonsense." Sam waved away her objection with the back of his hand. "The painting is yours. And I'll send you a print as soon as I can."

Kaylee felt a lump in her throat at his generosity. "I don't know what to say, except thank you, Mr. Miller."

"It's Sam. Merry Christmas, young lady."

"Thank you. Merry Christmas." Kaylee couldn't believe he'd given her such an incredible gift.

"You're most welcome." Sam smiled, then walked away to meet with other guests.

The door opened, and Kaylee looked to the front of the gallery.

Duncan stood there, surveying the room. The designer wore white sunglasses with reflective lenses, and he slid them back onto his forehead. A tropical print shirt peeked out from beneath his unbuttoned winter jacket. He made a beeline for Kaylee, Reese, and Nora, leaving curious glances in his wake. "Well hi, Kaylee."

Kaylee introduced Duncan to Nora and Reese, then asked, "What brings you here?"

"I asked at the inn if anything was going on tonight, and the lady at the desk said this was it." Duncan glanced around the room. "Nice shindig with lots of atmosphere. I'm impressed. It's quite a hopping party tonight."

Reese eyed the designer. "It's probably pretty tame compared to where you're used to going."

Duncan shrugged. "I'll take what I can get. I didn't want to bother going to Seattle this weekend. This place totally has my interest right now. Anyway, I came by to share my exciting announcement. I just signed an agreement with a production company for my own TV show!"

"You don't say," Reese said. "That's an interesting coincidence."

"Coincidence?" Duncan responded. "Oh, because of Kris. I get it. Look, I have no idea if his show is even going to air. All they've done is a pilot, and who knows what they'll do with it? But it's local, with a Seattle-based producer."

"Congratulations. So what will your show be about?" Kaylee asked.

"It'll be called *Duncan on Design.*" He spread his arms in the air as if displaying a sign. "I'm going to teach people how to add international decorating flair to their ho-hum homes."

"Well, that will definitely be interesting." Kaylee wasn't sure viewers would appreciate him calling their homes ho-hum, but she kept the observation to herself.

"I've already talked to Sierra, and she promised to make an announcement about the show on the night of the auction." Duncan rubbed his hands together at the prospect of free publicity.

"That's good. I'm sure they'll do something to honor Kris as well," Kaylee said.

Duncan rolled his eyes. "That man is still competing with me. Well, we've got a week until the big event." He stared over the top of Kaylee's head. "We'll talk more later. Gotta run." With that, he plunged into the crowd.

Nora shook her head as she watched him leave. "My, what a character. Definitely the artistic type."

"You can say that again." Reese grimaced. "Did you get the feeling that he wasn't really listening to anything anyone else said?"

Kaylee didn't answer, but Nora laughed.

"I need to refill the punch bowl. Enjoy, you two," Nora said, then headed to the refreshment area.

Kaylee heard a buzz coming from her purse, so she pulled out her phone. Jessica. She ignored it. She'd give her a call when she got home.

A few moments later, her phone buzzed again. What on earth?

This time it was a text from Jessica: *Do an Internet search for Meghan Benson Designs. Then call me.*

8

If Reese noticed Kaylee's distraction after she'd received Jessica's text, he didn't mention it. For the rest of the evening Kaylee nibbled on appetizers and enjoyed light chatter with Nora and the others at the gallery.

When Kaylee and Reese said good night to Nora and Christian, Nora promised to call Kaylee when the painting of The Flower Patch was ready to pick up. Kaylee still couldn't believe Sam Miller was giving her the beautiful painting, especially when she knew what it was worth.

Kaylee and Reese talked about the auction as they headed back to Wildflower Cottage.

"Thank you," she told Reese as he parked in the driveway. "I really enjoyed getting out for something not work related, if only for a few hours. Although I love my job and this business."

"I was glad to take you." He jumped out, rounded the truck, and opened her door.

As Reese walked her to the front door of the cottage, Kaylee reminded herself once more that this wasn't a real date and Reese was just being a gentleman.

"Thanks again," she said as she unlocked the door.

Bear bounded out to greet them as soon as she opened the door, and they laughed.

"Let me know when you're ready to start on the arrangements and displays at the mansion. I'll be there." Reese flashed her a grin before returning to his truck.

After letting Bear out and getting into her pajamas, Kaylee

finally settled down with a cup of tea in front of her laptop. Bear flopped over her feet and fell asleep.

She typed *Meghan Benson Designs* into the search engine. The first result was Kristopher Carroll's website.

Kris had a lovely site, with classic tones and a hint of Christmas. He clearly used his Santa look and his name as part of his brand but not to the extent that it was hokey. Meghan was listed as his assistant designer, with her photo and bio given on the website as well. There was nothing remarkable there.

Kaylee clicked back to the main search engine results, then skimmed several news articles about Kris that mentioned Meghan. The pair worked as a team, but Kris was the star of the show. The designer and his assistant seemed to have the normal dynamic for such an arrangement.

She returned to the search results page and found nothing that stood out or appeared suspicious. On the second page of the results she clicked on another link for *Meghan Benson Designs*, and a collection of photos and digital sketches popped up.

Meghan's work was good. Really good. Her style was a blend of contemporary with rustic touches, and she wasn't afraid to use color or flowers. Bea would love the arrangement with the ferns and lilies.

Kaylee closed the website and took a sip of her tea. "Bear, my little buddy, I don't see what Jess wanted me to find."

Bear's paw twitched in a dream.

Maybe it was another of Jessica's theories. The woman could spot a conspiracy a mile away, and if there wasn't one, she was adept at coming up with fresh theories all her own.

Kaylee grabbed her phone and called Jessica.

Her friend answered after the first ring. "Did you search for Meghan Benson Designs?" she demanded.

"Yes, but I didn't find anything incriminating."

"Look at Meghan's design portfolio," Jessica urged. "It mirrors Kris's portfolio on his website exactly."

Kaylee clicked on Kris's website portfolio, then opened another screen on her laptop and clicked on Meghan's portfolio. "I've opened their portfolios." She scanned both of them. "You're right. Did she lift his ideas?"

"It sure looks like it. But maybe it was the other way around," Jessica suggested. "Perhaps Meghan was the brains behind Kris's designs."

"Kris was his own creative genius," Kaylee stated. "He didn't need her to make his work. And it's clear he was in charge."

"Maybe at some point, the student became the master."

"If that's the case, then who's to say Meghan wasn't trying to strike out on her own?"

"Good point." Jessica was quiet for a moment. "Oh, and one of the articles said that Kris was developing memory problems. And did you read the article mentioning that Meghan wasn't going to be included in Kris's new TV show?"

"No, I didn't find that one."

"Well, there's a quote from Meghan saying that she was excited for her boss and mentor getting this once-in-a-lifetime opportunity," Jessica explained. "What if Meghan resented him leaving her behind and doing the show without her?"

"But it would be foolish for Kris to go on without her if in fact she is running his business," Kaylee pointed out.

"On the interior design shows that I've seen all the designers have assistants by their side," Jessica said. "Kris could have chosen another assistant instead of Meghan."

"So maybe she was angry at Kris for using her skills, then replacing her with someone else when he landed his own show. Meghan could have demanded a cut of the money as a type of severance. I bet those shows pay pretty nicely per episode if a series takes off."

They both fell silent for a moment.

"What if Meghan did something to Kris?" Jessica said in a low voice.

Kaylee thought about it. "You might be onto something. After all, she was the one who said that Kris told her to start working at the mansion without him because he wasn't feeling well."

"And that was the morning you found his body," Jessica said.

"But why would Meghan get rid of her ticket to continued success?"

"They could have argued about the show and their partnership, and she decided to take care of him once and for all."

Kaylee chuckled. "Were you a fan of Nancy Drew mysteries way back when?"

"Hey, don't knock the Girl Detective. I have several first editions on my bookshelf that I won't part with."

"If it makes you feel better," Kaylee said, "I'll talk to Nick about the websites and portfolios and see what he has to say. Maybe the police have already cleared Meghan. I don't know." Lately she'd had plenty on her plate with the general busyness of the Christmas season. She'd thought little about what was going on in the investigation and didn't envy Nick and the others with a case like this, especially at Christmastime.

"Thank you. I'd love it if you would. Sometimes I feel like I have an overactive imagination."

"I would never have guessed that of someone who has a geranium named Oliver that forecasts gloom," Kaylee said wryly.

"Very funny," Jessica said. "Well, I know tomorrow is a busy day at the shop, so I'll let you go."

"I'll be in touch if Nick has any information he can share."

Kaylee pulled away from the last delivery of the morning, this one in Eastsound. She'd just checked in with Mary at The Flower Patch. Mary assured her the morning had been slow except for a few phone calls, one of those from a nervous bride who was worried about her bouquets for the following weekend. Mary would be taking the lead on that project, but Kaylee would help deliver the flowers and set up. It would make a nice break from the open house at the mansion.

Kaylee glanced over at Bear riding shotgun. Strapped into his doggy seat belt, he raised his nose to sniff the fresh air coming in through the window. Kaylee had cracked it open just for him, as the day was mild for December.

Since she was already in Eastsound, she headed for the sheriff's department to talk to Nick. She wasn't sure if he was in the office today, but it wouldn't hurt to check. Last night after her conversation with Jessica, she'd wondered if her friend's seemingly outlandish ideas had any truth behind them.

Then there was the flamboyant Duncan getting his own show. Would his show succeed on its own, or had he decided to get rid of his competition? Not that Kris would have been competition for Duncan, whose show wasn't even in production yet. But somehow Kaylee doubted Duncan would have seen it that way.

Kaylee arrived at the sheriff's department and parked. She headed inside, carrying Bear and straightening his polka-dot bow tie.

Aida greeted Kaylee with a smile and a fresh burst of mint. "Well, hello there, you two. You here to see Deputy Durham, Sheriff Maddox, or both?"

"Deputy Durham. I happened to be in the area today. Is he around?" Kaylee asked.

"You're in luck. He's pulling a Saturday shift. I'll let him know you're here. Go on back." Aida gestured toward the door, then took a sip of coffee.

Nick looked up and smiled when he saw Kaylee and Bear in his office doorway. "Ah, good. I was planning to call you. There are a few more sets of samples at Akin's. Do you have time to analyze them?"

"Sure. What have you learned from the samples I've already examined?"

Nick leaned forward in his chair, resting his elbows on the desk. "Well, we've confirmed Mr. Carroll died somewhere else but was moved to the mansion not long after he died. As for the bullet, it does match the caliber of the gun Mrs. Roberts found in the Dumpster behind her shop."

"Who's the gun registered to?"

He gave a wry grin and shook his head. "I can't tell you that. We're assembling the case and working on warrants, which could mean more vegetation samples that will come your way. If I tell you who we suspect, you might look for evidence that proves guilt or innocence, instead of providing an objective analysis."

"I understand. I wouldn't want to do anything that would jeopardize the investigation." Kaylee didn't venture to be anything other than a forensic botanist. "I came by because—well, it almost sounds silly now, but Jess and I were talking about a theory last night as to who could have done—whatever was done to Mr. Carroll."

Nick motioned to the empty chair across from his desk. "Please sit down. I'll listen to it. I value your insight."

She settled onto the chair with Bear on her lap. The chair

squeaked as if it remembered her from the last time she visited the office.

It took Kaylee all of two minutes to tell Nick about what Jessica found online and the questions that came up when looking at both Meghan's and Kris's portfolios.

She took a deep breath when she was done. "I know it's probably circumstantial, and maybe you've already looked at what we found, but Jess really wanted me to tell you about it."

Nick wore a bemused expression. "You're right. It all sounds very circumstantial. But it's a place to start. We won't discount any of this as a possible lead."

"Thank you. I appreciate it."

"Ms. Benson has had to travel to Seattle to tend to some business affairs, and at this point, I'm not restricting her from leaving briefly. You can trust we're looking into Mr. Carroll's financials, his personal life, everything. It takes time. It's a process. And sometimes it's tedious."

Kaylee promised Nick she'd head over to Akin Funeral Chapel that afternoon. She'd originally planned to spend time at the mansion taking new photographs and rethinking her design. But the idea of seeing what new discoveries awaited under the microscope intrigued her more than the idea of designing a new arrangement.

When she returned to Turtle Cove, she dropped Bear off at The Flower Patch. Then she grabbed burgers and fries at the Pacific Street Diner for her and Mary and one cupcake apiece from Death by Chocolate.

Jessica looked a bit crestfallen after Kaylee told her about Nick's casual interest in Jessica's ideas.

"Cheer up, Nancy Drew. Nick will get to the bottom of things."

"I know, but I was hoping we'd crack the case." Jessica glanced over at Oliver. "Just look at him. He's downright dejected. The bad news isn't over."

A trio of ladies came in, visiting for the day from Seattle, chattering about how much they adored the quaint shops in Turtle Cove but expressing eagerness to rest their feet after Christmas shopping downtown.

"Death by Chocolate is the best name ever for a sweets shop," one of them said to Jessica.

Kaylee waved good-bye to her friend, who was displaying the éclairs, scones, and other treats ready to be devoured by the tourists, and returned to The Flower Patch.

Kaylee and Mary sat down to eat their lunch, and Kaylee tried to ignore Bear, who was at her feet and begging for a fry.

"So, I found out something interesting today," Mary announced before she took a bite of her burger.

"What's that?"

"Barbara and Kris weren't really engaged after all. Not officially, anyway."

"What?" Kaylee exclaimed. Good thing she didn't have any food in her mouth. She'd likely have choked on it.

Mary nodded. "Barbara's sister, Bernice, arrived in town today. I heard her talking at the market. She told the cashier that she was worried about Barbara, taking Kris's death so hard, even going so far as to claim they were engaged."

Kaylee pondered that for a moment. "Yes, I guess talking about an engagement that never happened would be considered taking his death very hard, a manifestation of grief. Maybe Barbara was speaking figuratively about them getting married. That she'd hoped to marry him someday."

"I'm not so sure she wasn't flat-out lying," Mary admitted. "She said they were planning to announce it at the open house, and we all assumed Kris had already popped the question because of the ring on her finger. None of us suspected grief-stricken wishful thinking on her part."

"I remember she told us they were engaged. But maybe her sister is right. Maybe Barbara is so upset over Kris that she made it up."

"Grief does make people do strange things, and appearances can be deceiving." Mary looked thoughtful for a moment.

"But that gigantic diamond on her finger. Where did it come from?"

"Bernice said it's only costume jewelry. Very convincing costume jewelry." Mary took a sip of tea, then continued. "I wonder if anyone's planned a memorial service or something."

"I haven't heard anything new since Sierra told us she had asked but didn't have the funds to do it." Kaylee dipped her fry in ketchup and popped it into her mouth.

The chime over the front door sounded.

Mary stood, motioning for Kaylee to stay seated. "Hold all those thoughts. I'll be back."

"Actually I should get going." Kaylee felt the urge to get over to the funeral chapel and see about those samples. She could ponder as she worked. She covered up the rest of her lunch and stuck it in the small refrigerator, the only one in the shop not dedicated to flowers.

She left Mary showing an older woman a collection of Christmas-themed table centerpieces while Bear discreetly sniffed at the woman's handbag. Not for the first time did Kaylee give thanks for Mary. She couldn't have learned the ropes of the business without her.

Two vehicles were in the parking lot of the funeral home when Kaylee pulled in. The back of her neck prickled when she opened one of the glass front doors and heard a shrill voice echoing the hall.

"What do you mean, his body hasn't been released yet?" Barbara demanded. "I want to hold a memorial service for him."

Kaylee heard Giles Akin's soothing tones as he responded. Although she didn't quite catch all the words, she heard him say something about "not being authorized at the moment."

Thelma Akin, Giles's wife, greeted Kaylee with a warm, wide smile. "Good afternoon. It's good to see you again. Giles is in his office." She cocked her head in the direction of the hallway and listened.

"I don't know if that's acceptable," Barbara snapped.

Thelma shook her head. "Oh my, now that doesn't sound good. You're welcome to go on back to the preparation room. Giles has everything ready. I know he would have liked to greet you, but he's a little busy at the moment."

Kaylee thanked Thelma, then proceeded down the hall. *A made-up engagement complete with a fake ring, and now Barbara is throwing a fit because Kris's body hasn't been released yet. Is she trying to hide something?*

9

Kaylee continued down the hallway toward the funeral home's preparation room.

As she passed Giles's office, he called out to her.

She put on her best smile as she stopped in the doorway and said hello.

Giles looked surprisingly unruffled behind his desk compared to Barbara, who wore a thundercloud expression. "Good afternoon, Kaylee."

"I spoke with Deputy Durham, and he said you have more samples ready for me to analyze," Kaylee explained.

Barbara turned to Kaylee. "Samples?"

Kaylee glanced from Barbara to Giles. "I'm assisting the sheriff's department in the investigation surrounding Mr. Carroll's death."

"Whatever qualifies *you* to do such a thing?" Barbara looked her up and down. "I didn't know you were a police officer or a CSI person."

"I'm not. I'm a plant taxonomist," Kaylee said. "If there's any type of vegetation or plant matter that was found at the scene or on or around Mr. Carroll, I'll know what it is."

"And we are very grateful for your assistance," Giles said.

"I'm happy to provide it." Kaylee stood a bit taller.

Barbara's features softened. "Well, good. The sooner they find out who did this to him, the better."

"That's what I'm hoping to do. Or at least help point them in the right direction." Kaylee turned to Giles. "I'll be in the prep room."

He nodded. "The room is free until four. Let me know if

you need anything."

As Kaylee left the office, she heard Giles continue with Barbara. "I've been able to sign off on the death certificate, but I'm awaiting clearance from the authorities to release Mr. Carroll's remains. If you would like to hold a memorial, you can still do so. You're welcome to have the service here."

So, Giles had signed a death certificate, which meant he had identified a cause of death. What was that cause?

She entered the prep room and headed for the microscope, shifting her focus to where it needed to be for the next couple of hours. She had bigger things to take care of today than thinking about what was written on Kristopher Carroll's death certificate. *Or smaller things, actually*, she mused.

A fresh set of sample containers waited on the stainless steel table. Kaylee brought the notepad Giles had given her to use last time, and she also pulled out her phone so she could record her thoughts on the voice recorder as she studied the samples.

One container was marked *beard*.

She avoided contemplating where the samples had been taken from and instead focused on trying to find out the facts regarding what she would examine. It was a sliver of something green, which had a faint tint of brown.

Kaylee pushed the button on the recorder and took verbal notes. "I'm looking at a sample from Mr. Carroll's beard. It appears to be from a type of conifer of the family *Pinaceae*. The slivers are no longer than half a centimeter, green in color with tinges of brown. It is my belief they came from a real, not artificial, pine tree."

"I have another vial for you," Giles said, suddenly appearing at her elbow. "This is one I meant to have on the table last time. Unfortunately, it was left in the refrigerator by mistake."

Kaylee tried not to jump. Giles sure had a knack for sneaking up on a person. "Thank you." She accepted a vial marked *stomach* from him.

He slipped away as noiselessly as he'd arrived.

Kaylee squinted at the vial and saw flecks of something inside a clear liquid. She fished out some of the flecks with a tiny blotting strip and placed them on a slide, then popped it into the microscope.

The sample images came into focus. It was a plant she hadn't seen in a while—*Nicotiana tabacum*, also known as tobacco.

She'd seen chewing tobacco before. But most people didn't swallow it. Not on purpose, anyway. However, would the amount in Kris's stomach have been enough to kill him? She'd have to find out how much tobacco was inside his stomach overall. She also didn't recall anyone mentioning Kris having a habit of chewing tobacco. If he did, it would have been nearly impossible to hide given his beard, which was snowy white and always kept impeccably groomed.

Kaylee then reminded herself she'd been given one job in this investigation, and that was to identify the samples collected for her by both Giles along with the sheriff's department, not to try to figure out what had happened.

"Jess is rubbing off on me," she muttered.

Kaylee finished recording her notes so she could take them home and type up her findings for the sheriff.

One sample she'd found the first time still poked at the back of her mind. It wasn't one of the vegetative samples but the royal blue thread.

It begged an answer to the question: Where had Kris Carroll been when he died?

As Kaylee left the funeral chapel, she realized that it would be a good time to stop by the mansion for another look around. It was open today, with a group of student volunteers helping to give the place some spit and polish before the big night.

When she arrived at the mansion, she found about ten students working diligently to clean the mansion under the direction of their group leader. Some of the students were seniors in high school and could possibly be among the first recipients of the scholarships presented at Friday night's open house and auction.

Kaylee stepped around a sign denoting a wet floor beside the stairs and strolled from room to room. The pungent smell of wood soap filled her nose. She searched for royal blue carpeting but didn't see any. Nothing struck her as out of the ordinary either.

If only they could get answers to banish some of the pall hanging over the House of Christmas Trees event. Not that they should ignore Kris's passing, but it was hard to think of and enjoy the open house without remembering its intended star, whose bright light had been extinguished much too soon.

She headed down the hallway to the rear of the mansion. Opening the back door, she took in the sight of the dormant rose gardens, still crusty with the frozen dampness of the morning.

Kaylee went outside and closed the door behind her. She gazed around the perimeter of the property. A tall hedge and a stone fence enclosed the entire area. She'd heard somewhere that the fence was made of rough-hewn New Hampshire granite hauled in about one hundred years before, a sign of status back in the day.

This garden offered quick access into the mansion. Kaylee realized that in the darkness of night, the hedge and the fence would provide good cover. Someone could easily pass through here unnoticed. She walked the path, stopping every so often to see if there was any sign that something—like a body—had been dragged through the area recently.

She paused at a rosebush, bereft of leaves. Something bright and man-made against the dull winter colors caught her eye. Blue threads and they looked familiar. Kaylee took pictures with her phone to record exactly where the threads were. She didn't have a bag, so she extracted an empty envelope from her purse. Using the envelope's flap, she carefully removed a thread from the lower part of a branch. It wasn't perfect and most likely not worthy of *CSI*, but it would do. All she needed was one thread.

Kaylee refolded the envelope and tucked it into her purse. She'd drop it off at the sheriff's department so they could see if it matched the blue thread that had been found on Kris's boot.

She continued along the path. It led to a gate that opened up onto a backstreet. The rear access of several businesses faced the back of the mansion. It probably wasn't the view that the mansion's original property owners had envisioned.

Stopping at the gate, Kaylee scanned the street, which was quiet today. It would have been easy enough for someone to drive up here at night, without the headlights on, unload a body, then drag it into the mansion. Well, not easy. But it could be done if someone was strong enough or if someone dragged the body on a tarp. *Or perhaps on a blue rug.*

Kaylee shivered. She was gaining nothing by standing out here in the cold, so she turned and trudged back to the rear entrance of the mansion. As she did so, some wood stacked near the steps snagged her attention. The straight, round logs could have helped someone drag a weight along the path, then up the steps. If people used the laws of physics and the right tools, they could move a weight far greater than themselves.

Kaylee laughed at herself. She'd tell Jessica about her sleuthing later after dropping the sample off at the sheriff's department.

As she passed through the mansion, she studied the floor

and the lower parts of period furniture, such as the legs on the short table next to the door of the storage closet where Kris had been found. Nothing clung to the legs of the mahogany piece. However, if there had been threads stuck to the table's legs, they'd likely been removed with all the cleaning and dusting that had gone on, both after the break-in and today in preparation for the open house.

When Kaylee reentered the grand entryway hall, she found Meghan staring forlornly at the spot where a large Christmas tree was to be placed next week. It was a replacement for the tree the vandals had destroyed.

Kaylee moved to stand beside her. "My offer is still good to help you on Thursday during setup."

"Thank you." Her tone was flat.

"Is there something wrong?"

Meghan frowned. "I found out more bad news today."

"I'm sorry to hear that," Kaylee said. "Do you want to talk about it?"

"I'm not sure if I should." Meghan glanced around, then lowered her voice. "When I left on the ferry a few days ago, it wasn't to take care of business for Carroll Design." She took a deep breath. "To be completely honest with you, I had a job interview. It was something I'd set up before I came to Turtle Cove."

"What do you mean?" Kaylee asked. "Kris let you go?"

Meghan nodded. "After this event, I'm out of a job. Technically speaking, since this is a volunteer job Kris was paying me an honorarium for, I'm out of work now."

"When did this happen?"

"I knew things were on the outs with Kris for a while. He wanted someone fast to help him, who can climb on things, move furniture, stage, and all of that. Well, he'd already picked someone. Not me. I'm not even thirty yet, and he thought I was getting old." Her shoulders sank.

"I'm sorry." Kaylee touched her arm. "You're a brilliant designer. Your career is definitely not over."

"Thank you. Kris's new protégée is named Brittney. Or was. I mean, her name's the same, but she's not a protégée anymore." Meghan's face flushed. "She's fresh out of design school and nimble as a cat, or so I've been told. I just couldn't believe Kris was replacing me after all the years of dedication I put into his company. So I had to leave the island to see about that job. To give myself a future."

"Deputy Durham cleared you to leave the island."

"Yes, but I didn't tell him it was for a job interview because I don't want any of this to get out. I did nothing to cause Kris's death, but I know how small communities are. How the design community is. People will talk. They'll say I was mad at him, and I was responsible for it."

"I won't say anything about this. You have my word," Kaylee assured her. "But you must promise me you'll tell Deputy Durham the real reason why you left. I wouldn't be surprised if he already knows the state of affairs at Carroll Design. It wouldn't look good for you if the police found out that you hid something from them."

Voices came closer, and Kaylee recognized one of them. Sierra and a trio of teenagers entered the hall.

Sierra greeted Kaylee, but she didn't say anything to Meghan. "What brings you here, Kaylee?"

"I'm just looking around, mentally getting ready for the open house." Kaylee knew that was true. Her curiosity had also led her to find the rose garden and the path at the rear of the mansion. But she didn't add that bit of information.

The front door to the mansion opened, and Deputy Nick Durham strode inside, his face as serious as a stone. He stopped short of the three women. "Miss Underwood, I need to speak to you for a moment. Outside if you don't mind."

"You can talk with me here," Sierra said, but her voice trembled. "I don't have anything to hide."

"Okay then." Nick glanced at Kaylee and Meghan, then faced Sierra. "Miss Underwood, do you own a gun?"

"Yes I do." Her forehead wrinkled.

Nick nodded. "Then I need you to come with me to the sheriff's department to give a statement."

Kaylee stood there, unsure of what to make of the situation. *The gun Jess found belongs to Sierra?*

The students who'd witnessed the brief conversation murmured as Sierra followed Nick out of the mansion.

Sierra hesitated on the steps. "Kaylee, can you shut everything down and lock up for me? The kids are pretty much done. I've got the key. Please hang on to it."

"I can do that." Kaylee hurried over and accepted the key.

Then Kaylee and Meghan helped the teens gather up the cleaning supplies, dump the water from the mop buckets down the drain, and store the vacuum cleaner in the supply closet.

"I think we're done for the day, everyone. You can call your parents and go home," Kaylee announced. "I know Miss Underwood is very grateful for all your help."

"Miss Underwood owns a *gun*?" one of the boys commented. "Hard core."

"Which means nobody will mess with Miss Underwood," another boy said.

"Unless you're with the police department," a young brunette whispered.

After the students left, a vehicle careened into the mansion's parking lot, and Barbara burst from it. She all but bounded in their direction, her arms swinging. A large tote bag bounced on her hip.

"I'm here to get some work done while it's quiet." Barbara scaled the steps and stopped in the doorway. "My sister's visiting, and she's talking so much I can't think straight. I told her I needed to work on my project."

"The dining room is ready and waiting for you." Kaylee handed the key to Barbara.

But the older woman pressed it back into Kaylee's hand. "I don't need it. Sierra gave me a spare the other day. She said she'd made an extra one for the open house, with the owner's permission." Barbara's expression appeared the brightest since before they'd found Kris in the closet.

Kaylee nodded and slipped the key into her purse.

Meghan headed for the front steps. "Ladies, I'll see you Thursday, if not sooner. Kaylee, I've thought of another concept I'd like to use on the main display. I'll e-mail it to you and let you know what I need for a supply list."

Barbara put her hands on her hips. "Aren't you presumptuous? You leave Kris's design alone. Keep it exactly the way he had it."

Meghan rolled her eyes as she turned away.

"Don't roll your eyes at me," Barbara snapped. "I happen to have a copy of Kris's design, so I know what it's supposed to look like. It *will* stay the way he had it, or I'll fix it myself."

"Whatever. I'm not that heartless." Meghan's eyes brimmed with tears. "I cared about Kris. He was like a—"

"Don't say father," Barbara spat.

Meghan glared at Barbara. "I was going to say *uncle*. He was like an uncle to me. I plan to honor him with his last design. It will be the best thing he's ever done."

"Ladies, please," Kaylee interjected. She'd encountered temperamental professors during her years at the university, but none of them held a candle to temperamental, dramatic interior designers.

The two women stopped glaring at each other and turned softer expressions on her.

Kaylee cleared her throat. "Monday morning I'm placing one more floral order that will arrive before the open house," she said, changing the subject. "If there is anything you need, please let me know by Sunday night. I prefer if you e-mail me your lists so I can reference them as needed."

Both Barbara and Meghan nodded, but neither of them said anything, though Kaylee thought she felt the tension in the room lessen.

"I'm sure you have wholesalers you work with," she continued. "But if you order with me, all you'll have to pay is my cost because I have an agreement with my supplier for regular delivery, so it would save you a delivery charge."

"All right, thank you," Meghan said. "I'll keep that in mind."

Kaylee turned her focus to Barbara. "I heard you talking with Mr. Akin earlier this afternoon. About a memorial for Kris."

Barbara's cheeks flushed. "I'm afraid I was a bit upset. It's been a difficult week, to say the least. I want to do *something*. Kris set aside his time and his own interests to do something for the kids in this town. It meant so much for him to be here. You just don't know—"

"You've suffered a loss, Barbara, and I'm sorry," Kaylee said. "Let me know what you plan to do, and I'll be glad to provide flowers or table arrangements. Whatever you need."

"Thank you. I'm planning to reserve the private dining room at The Ideal Meal. I'm opening the memorial to the community and whoever would like to come. I've thought of a short program. And I have some photos."

"I can send you some pictures," Meghan said. "Whenever Kris designed a project or while we were setting up a new room,

I took pictures. It bugged him sometimes, I think. But I explained that people enjoy seeing how a design comes together."

"You're right. And yes, I'd like very much to use those pictures." Barbara put her arm around Meghan. "I'm sorry I've been so difficult. Kris really did think the world of you."

Meghan smiled through her tears. "Thank you."

With the other two women seemingly on the way to burying whatever hatchet had been between them, Kaylee figured now was a good time to leave. Her first priority was to head over to the sheriff's department and drop off the blue thread she'd taken from the mansion's yard. Then she could go to The Flower Patch, check in with Mary once more, and take Bear home for supper.

As Kaylee approached her vehicle, she spotted something small and white tucked under the windshield wiper. She scanned the parking lot. No one was around. Kaylee picked up a folded piece of paper and opened it.

Mind your own business. Stop helping the police. Or else.

10

"Well, fancy seeing you here again so soon," Aida said when Kaylee entered the sheriff's department.

"Is Deputy Durham still in, by chance?" Kaylee asked.

"I'm afraid he's unavailable right now." Aida pointed at the envelope in Kaylee's hands. "What do you have there?"

"It's something I picked up that I'd like him to see. I've written a note on the envelope, explaining what's inside." Kaylee tried to keep her hands from shaking as she thought of the threatening note she also held with the envelope.

"Well, Deputy Garcia is here," Aida said. "I'm sure she can help you. I know she's been working with him. Let me buzz her."

The deputy met Kaylee at the reception desk, then led her to the offices. "Okay, Kaylee, what can I help you with?"

"Two things." Kaylee held up the envelope and the note. "I was in the backyard at the mansion today and found some blue threads stuck on a rosebush. I'm wondering if they're the same as what was found on Mr. Carroll's boot."

"All right." Deputy Garcia took the envelope from her. "We'll get this labeled and logged in, and then I'll check them out. What else do you have for me?"

"Before I left the mansion, I found this note on my windshield," Kaylee told her. "Someone's warning me that I need to stop helping you in this investigation."

"Hold on a sec." Deputy Garcia left the room and returned a moment later carrying a plastic bag. "Stick the note in here. I'll check it out too."

Kaylee slipped the note into the bag, then explained, "Deputy Durham arrived before I left and asked Sierra to come with him. They were gone by the time I got out to my vehicle, or I would have shown him the note right away."

"No problem," Deputy Garcia said. "How long were you at the mansion?"

"Forty-five minutes or so."

"Who did you see there?"

"Well, a group of high school students was there with Sierra Underwood," Kaylee replied. "Meghan Benson and Barbara Lang-Masters were there too."

"Do all of them know you've been working for us?" Deputy Garcia asked.

"Yes, I'm sure they do. Except for the students, I guess. At any rate, I haven't kept it a secret."

"Did you see anyone in the parking lot when you found the note?"

Kaylee shook her head. "There was no one else around."

Deputy Garcia sealed the bag and wrote on its label. "If you're not comfortable working for us anymore on this particular case, it's completely understandable. I'm sure Deputy Durham would agree with me. If you don't feel safe, we wouldn't blame you if you stopped."

"I must admit that seeing the note on my windshield threw me a little bit." Kaylee gave an involuntary shudder. "Other than the note, I haven't felt like anyone's been following me or paying attention to what I've been up to. But, no, I'm not going to stop. If there's any way I can help you, I will."

"We're really thankful for your assistance. We have a great department here, and we do what we can with what we have. But your expertise is invaluable."

"I'm glad that I can help," Kaylee said.

"Personally, I'd love to learn some pointers on botany," Deputy Garcia admitted.

"Well, I'd be glad to give you a few tips sometime."

"I appreciate that. I'll let you know if we find anything other than your prints on the note."

Kaylee thanked her, then hurried back to The Flower Patch to find Mary winding things down for the weekend. They would reopen on Monday.

Bear hurried across the sales floor to meet her, his tail whipping from side to side. She squatted down, and he hopped up to give her a wet, sloppy kiss.

She rubbed the dog's floppy ears, then stood. "Thank you, Mary."

Her friend looked up from the cash register, where she was closing out the transactions for the day. "For what?"

"You've been amazing, especially during this busy holiday season. I couldn't do it without you."

"I'm sure you'd find a way. But I'm happy to help." Mary paused. "Have you spoken to your grandmother lately?"

"Not since the other day when I talked to her about what happened to Kris."

Mary nodded. "I miss her. I know she's proud of you, though. And not to change the subject, but do you have plans for Christmas?"

Kaylee shook her head.

"Then come for dinner on Christmas Day. No one else is going to make it home this year, so it'll be just Herb and me. We're not planning anything big, but it'll be delicious. I can guarantee you that we'll have steak."

"I'd love that." Kaylee smiled. "Thank you."

Mary smiled too. "Plan to come at four. We'll have the fire lit."

"Sounds both lovely *and* relaxing."

"I think we've all earned a little relaxation, especially with the House of Christmas Trees chaos."

"I couldn't agree with you more. Should I bring anything?"

"Just bring yourself. And Bear, of course." Mary closed the register and handed Kaylee a plastic zippered bank bag for the deposit. "There. That's done."

"Thank you again."

Mary took her purse out from under the counter and slung the strap over her shoulder. "Don't forget the Petal Pushers are meeting tomorrow. It's the last gathering until after New Year's. We take a break over the holidays."

"I'll be there." Kaylee looked forward to trays of goodies, a cup of tea, and good conversation. There wasn't much actual gardening to do this time of year, but it was fun to plan for the spring and summer outdoor growing seasons.

"Can't wait to hear what Jess comes up with next for us to chew on," Mary said as she grabbed her coat and patted Bear good-bye. "And I don't mean something chocolate. Well, not just chocolate."

Kaylee laughed. With Jessica, one never knew.

The Petal Pushers gathered at the keeper's quarters in the Old Cape Lighthouse the next afternoon.

The get-together had the cheerful atmosphere of a Christmas party with all the treats to go along with it. Jessica brought miniature chocolate cheesecake tarts, chocolate truffles, tiny molten chocolate cake bites that oozed a delightfully fudgy ganache, and a carafe of hot chocolate. Kaylee provided a platter of cheese and crackers, and Mary carried in a tray of fresh vegetables "to cancel out the sugar."

Bear lay contentedly at Kaylee's feet. He sported a bow tie dotted with miniature poinsettias and was busily chewing one of the homemade dog treats Mary gave him.

"Can't leave out our little guy," Mary had said when she presented Kaylee with a plastic bag containing a handful of tiny bone-shaped dog cookies.

DeeDee's contribution for the meeting was a plate of cookies that looked like carefully arranged store-bought baking. "I'm sorry the cookies are not homemade, but I'm not that sorry." She took a sip of hot chocolate. "On top of the regular holiday craziness, the girls still have a few more days of school, we're deep-cleaning the house before Andy's parents get here, and I have some soap orders yet to ship out. So we don't have time to start baking until next week."

Jessica nibbled on a cheesecake tart. "Not a problem at all. We're just glad you're here."

"I'm glad I'm here too. It always seems like everything is in overdrive during the last week before Christmas, and I don't like it." DeeDee reached for a cookie. "I have nothing wrapped yet. I think I remember where Andy and I hid the girls' presents, but I'm not 100 percent sure. Maybe 50 percent."

The others laughed.

"It's easy to find ourselves busy. Just look at everything we do," Kaylee commented. She'd stayed up late, typing the report of her most recent analysis of the samples collected by the sheriff's department.

"Like Friday night dates." Jessica gave Kaylee a sideways glance. "So, how did it go?"

"You had a date?" Mary's eyebrows shot up.

Kaylee braced herself to be grilled on her evening out with Reese. "It wasn't a date."

"What was it then?" Mary asked. "Tell us all about it."

Kaylee grabbed a carrot stick and swirled it in a little pool of dip on her plate. "There's not much to tell. We went to O'Brien's and had a great dinner, then stopped by the opening at Art Attack."

DeeDee grinned. "Sounds like a date to me. Now, if I could get Andy to do that on a Friday night once in a while . . ."

"Did you have a good time?" Mary asked.

Kaylee crunched on her carrot and swallowed the bite before responding. "Yes. I was happy to go out. It was a nice change of pace from staying home. Not that I'm lonely. I have you and Bear and all the other wonderful people I've gotten to know here in town."

Thankfully, the conversation shifted to the weekend ahead, with the House of Christmas Trees. But before that, there was the matter of Kristopher Carroll's memorial service.

"Barbara is having it at Death by Chocolate, as she informed me that The Ideal Meal's private dining room is already booked due to a holiday party," Jessica announced. "I'm thankful for the business."

"I thought she was planning something a little more, shall we say, fancy? Not that your place isn't spectacular, but from the way Barbara was going on about a memorial, it sounded as if she wanted something more over the top." Mary snagged a truffle. "Like a catered meal, a string trio playing in the background, and speeches." She shook her head. "I'm sorry. I'm not trying to sound insensitive."

"Of course not," Kaylee said. "I agree. When is the memorial?"

"Wednesday at two o'clock," Jessica said. "Barbara ordered two dozen of almost everything on my menu. We'll have enough food to feed Turtle Cove, if not the island. She's bringing in a projector to show a video of some kind, and I am positive she's written a speech."

The door to the meeting room swung open.

Bear, who'd been dozing at Kaylee's feet, let out a bark as he was startled from sleep.

Sierra stood in the doorway. "Ladies, I'm sorry for interrupting, but can I come in for a few minutes?"

Kaylee couldn't hide her surprise. The last time she'd seen Sierra was at the mansion the previous afternoon when Nick had showed up to ask her to come to the sheriff's department. She glanced at her friends' faces. They looked just as surprised as she was.

Mary recovered first. "Come on in. And no apology necessary." She tapped the empty chair next to her. "Get yourself a plate too."

Sierra pulled out the chair Mary had indicated and sank onto it. "No thanks. I'm not planning to stay long, and I couldn't eat a bite anyway. I'm here to tell you I'm in trouble. Big trouble."

"Is it about the gun Deputy Durham mentioned yesterday?" Kaylee leaned forward in her chair.

Sierra nodded. "When I lived in the city, my house was broken into while I was at home. The robbers held me at gunpoint and threatened me. They took my cash, my computer, my TV. I was never so scared in all my life, and I never want to be that afraid again." She shuddered. "So I bought a gun a few years ago and learned how to use it."

"That's simply awful," Mary said. "I don't blame you for wanting some protection, especially since you live alone."

"Why did Deputy Durham talk to you about it?" Kaylee asked.

Sierra took a deep breath. "The gun Jessica found in the Dumpster was mine. They also told me that it was the same gun used to shoot Kris."

The Petals looked at each other in disbelief.

"I didn't shoot him." Sierra wrung her hands. "I should have reported it, but I didn't know."

"Didn't know what, honey?" DeeDee's tone was warm.

"My gun was stolen," Sierra replied.

"When did you notice it was missing?" Jessica asked.

"Well, at first I didn't notice because I hide it and I don't check it very often. But after Deputy Durham told me that my gun was used to shoot Kris, I knew it had been stolen. Then I remembered that the morning after the reception my door was ajar, so it must have been taken the night of the reception."

Mary frowned. "You didn't report a possible break-in to the police?"

"No. I thought maybe I'd forgotten to lock the door because I was so tired when I got home from the reception," Sierra said. "Sometimes the breeze can blow the door open. Even if the handle is locked, if you don't jiggle it, the latch won't catch."

"But why do they think you would shoot Kris?" Kaylee asked. "What would your motive be?"

"There's no way I would ever want to kill him." Sierra glanced around at each of them. "Kris was my father."

11

Kaylee gaped at Sierra as she tried to process the information. "Why didn't you tell us?"

"I didn't know until after my mother passed away. Kris broke the news to me himself." Sierra brushed a tear from her eye. "That's why he started spending so much time here and how he got to know Barbara. I wasn't too happy about them getting together because she's such a pill in general. But he said he wanted to get to know me too."

"But your mother," Jessica said. "What did she tell you about your dad?"

"He was out of the picture while I was growing up. My mother always told me he was someone she knew when he worked the fishing boats, back when they were younger. He was charming, funny, kind. Not a man to be tied down." Sierra shrugged. "It happens. I wasn't the first kid to grow up without a father, and I won't be the last. Mom and I didn't have much, but we were happy."

"Did Kris know about you when you were born?" Mary asked. "I can't imagine someone knowing they had a child and not at least attempting to be a part of her life."

"Kris said he didn't know about me until he received a letter from my mother when she was diagnosed with terminal cancer," Sierra explained.

"What a shock to find your father after so many years," DeeDee remarked. "How were you adjusting after you met?"

"Kris and I both wanted to go forward and get to know each other, not live in the past. I couldn't help but love him. He was very

adamant about helping to raise funds for student scholarships."
Sierra's voice cracked. "He didn't want them to have as hard of
a time as I did, trying to get through school."

Mary patted Sierra's hand. "I'm so sorry."

"Thank you. I'm not sure I've really processed everything
that's happened." Sierra wiped her eyes. "It all seems like a happy
dream sometimes. I should have known it would disappear."

Kaylee wanted to tell her that things would get better in
time. But she still had both of her parents and hadn't walked
in Sierra's shoes. Instead, she said, "We just need to believe
the sheriff's department will get to the bottom of what actually
happened to your father."

"I'm sure they will," DeeDee said. "They're very thorough."

Kaylee recalled Nick Durham's statement that they weren't
sure whether the gunshot had killed Kris. She also couldn't picture
the petite Sierra hauling a body into the mansion by herself, nor
could she picture the young woman shooting anyone. And then
another question that came around to her yet again: Why hide
the body in the mansion at all? In fact, what if the whole thing
with the gun was a setup? She stopped the flood of questions in
her mind and snapped her attention back to Sierra.

Mary glanced at Kaylee with concern. "What is it? You look
like you want to say something."

"Not really. I don't know. I have more questions than anything
else." But at the moment, Kaylee couldn't discuss her work in
analyzing the samples from Kris and the closet or the samples
she'd found at the mansion. Nick and the sheriff's department
trusted her, and she didn't want her good intentions to foul
anything up for them.

"I think you should get an attorney as soon as possible,"
DeeDee told Sierra.

The others agreed.

"I'll do that," Sierra promised.

"Get out ahead of this too," Jessica continued. "I've watched enough true crime shows to know that an investigation can get bad for innocent people."

"And I've read enough books to know that too," DeeDee interjected.

Sierra sighed. "I'm sorry to be such a downer at your Christmas party."

"Nonsense. We're glad you came to us. We understand the holidays haven't been easy for you this year, and now that we know about Kris . . ." Jessica picked up the box of chocolate truffles and passed it to Sierra. "Please have a truffle. Or two or three. However many."

"Thank you." After taking a truffle, Sierra bit into it and closed her eyes. "This is amazing."

"I'm convinced chocolate can't heal everything, but it's pretty medicinal sometimes," Jessica said sagely.

"I think anyone who's had your baking would be inclined to agree," Mary told her fondly.

The discussion shifted to the plans for the open house at the mansion. The designers would be working on-site all day Thursday to set up and build their displays, with some extra time allowed on Friday morning. There was a VIP tour planned for Friday afternoon, and the auction was set for that same night. The schedule nearly made Kaylee's head spin, but she looked forward to it.

"I just remembered," Kaylee said. "Sierra, I have the mansion key. I meant to return it to you sooner, but the weekend got away from me, and I didn't know if you were still at the police station." She took it from her purse's inner pocket and handed it to Sierra.

"I promised the owner that I wouldn't be passing keys around to everyone, so thanks for holding on to it for me." Sierra tucked the key into her own purse. "I assume you had no problem locking up on Saturday?"

"Actually, I didn't have to," Kaylee said. "Barbara came by to get some fresh inspiration for her room, as she put it, and she insisted on locking up with her own key."

Sierra looked like she wanted to say something, but she simply nodded.

"How is publicity going for the open house?" Mary asked. "I've been knee-deep in work, and I haven't heard any updates lately."

"I think it's going all right so far," Sierra said. "We've sold over 100 tickets at last count, and of course we expect a lot of people to buy tickets at the door. The tickets will at least cover the cost of the snacks and refreshments." She selected a miniature cheesecake and took a bite.

After Sierra left—with a paper plate piled high with goodies—Jessica put on her determined face, her jaw set, and turned to Kaylee. "I know you've been helping Deputy Durham and can't tell us anything about the official investigation, but I think we need to sniff out some answers on our own."

"I agree with you. It won't hurt to see if we can find some connections. Sierra needs all the help she can get," Kaylee said.

"Has anyone backtracked to figure out who was the last person to see Kris alive?" Jessica asked.

"I don't know for sure. But Meghan said she talked to Kris the night he wasn't feeling well," Kaylee said. "The current theory is that Kris's body was moved to that closet after he died."

"The reason we found him as soon as we did was because Meghan called his phone and the battery wasn't dead." Mary looked thoughtful. "Well, I'm sure the sheriff's department has been tracking where his phone was that night."

"But then," Kaylee ventured, "I don't know that the phone

towers can pinpoint exactly where his phone was. Just a general area. So if Kris was in Turtle Cove when he died, he could have been almost anywhere in town."

"Why didn't this person or persons take away his cell phone and hide it or destroy it?" DeeDee asked.

"Careless," Jessica said. "They were careless, pure and simple."

"Or maybe they didn't realize he had a phone on him," Mary suggested.

"Maybe whatever happened to Kris was an accident," Kaylee ventured.

"If that's the case, then why not simply call 911 and get him help?" Mary countered. "Why didn't they call the sheriff's department and explain what happened? Gunshot aside, that is."

"Because someone had too much to lose," Jessica said darkly.

They let the comment hang in the air between the four of them for a moment.

Jessica spoke up again. "We should ask around to see if anyone has photos from the reception. DeeDee, I know you and I weren't there. But, Mary and Kaylee, what do you remember from that night?"

Kaylee considered the evening carefully. She'd spent most of the time chatting with Mary and Herb. Then the reporter from the local newspaper had interviewed her and Mary, looking for a few quotes for his article.

"I talked to Meghan and Kris not long after I got there," Kaylee said. "It was about seven, because I came straight from The Flower Patch after closing. I went to the buffet table first—I was so hungry I was ready to eat a table leg—and that's where I first saw Kris. We talked about our room plans while we went through the buffet line, and I told him how excited I was to hear about his TV show and I couldn't wait to see it."

Next was Mary's turn. "Barbara cornered Herb and me and

talked our ears off until Kaylee came over to our rescue. After that, Barbara latched on to Kris for most of the time." She grinned. "Herb commented if that woman clamped Kris's arm any tighter it would lose circulation and fall off."

"Did either of you notice when Kris left?" Jessica asked.

"No." Kaylee thought for a second. "Wait—I do remember Duncan kept razzing Kris about his new show. He asked him how he'd keep ratings up if it wasn't Christmastime. Kris said people would watch him any time of the year. Then Kris said, 'At least I'm not a washed-up surfer who calls himself a designer because he painted a surfboard once. Throwing fishing nets and cork around willy-nilly isn't designing.' Duncan didn't appreciate those comments, as I'm sure you can all imagine."

Jessica picked up her phone. "Here's the event page online. Someone posted photos throughout the evening. Surely there's a way to form a timeline from this."

"Where did Kris stay in Turtle Cove?" Kaylee asked. "At Northern Lights Inn? Or with Barbara?"

"I know the answer to that one." DeeDee waved her hand in the air, as if she were in class. "He was staying at the inn. He stopped into the shop one day to pick up some books and told me the inn didn't have much in the way of reading material that interested him. Then he cleared me out of the paperback Westerns I had on hand."

"How close is the inn to the mansion?" Kaylee asked.

"Just a few minutes by car, I think," Mary said, punctuating her comment with a sigh. "Girls, if you don't mind, I make a motion that we table discussion of this whodunit until another time. Right now, we should focus on celebrating Christmas and the coming year."

"Hear, hear," Kaylee said, lifting her mug. "Here's to a merry Christmas and a happy New Year for everyone in Turtle Cove."

"I second." Jessica raised her own mug, then frowned. "Except Oliver is still droopy, and that doesn't bode well."

After a full day filling orders on Monday, Kaylee headed home to Wildflower Cottage. The day had been horribly long, so long in fact that her cell phone battery had died. *I really should start keeping a charger in my purse.*

Kaylee parked her vehicle and trudged to the house. Bear plodded along beside her. He'd had a big day for a little dog. She took the steps carefully because it was pitch-black, and she hadn't turned on the porch light when she'd run home earlier to grab lunch, not realizing she'd be home well after dark.

As she fumbled for her house key, she noticed a piece of paper tucked into her storm door. *Not again.* Kaylee snatched the note from the door, then tried to calm her racing heart while she worked the key in the lock. *There.*

She hurried inside with Bear, slamming the door behind them. The noise made her flinch, and Bear barked, startled.

Kaylee turned the dead bolt in the lock. "I'm sorry, boy. I'm just a little jumpy tonight."

Bear looked up at her with concern. At least that was what Kaylee read in his large brown eyes.

She strode into the kitchen and tossed her purse and keys on the table, then unfolded the note.

Can't you follow instructions? Leave well enough alone.

Or what? What would happen if she continued to help the police? Part of her believed it was an empty threat, but a larger part of her felt a bit rattled. She needed to report it right now.

Kaylee set the note down, then hurried to her charger on the coffee table and plugged her phone in. She found Nick's number in her contacts and made the call.

He answered right away. "Deputy Durham."

"Nick, it's Kaylee Bleu. I'm sorry to call you at night like this."

"No problem. What's going on?"

"When I got home a few minutes ago I found another anonymous note. It was tucked into my front door."

"What does it say?"

Kaylee picked up the note and read it to him. "I'm assuming it's the same writer because it's the same type of paper and handwriting as the other note I found on my windshield at the mansion."

"Well, I can tell you we found two different sets of prints on the note you gave us. One set belongs to you. Your prints are on file from your consulting work with the Seattle police."

"I remember. What about the other set?"

"We haven't identified it yet," Nick replied. "Now let's go back to a few minutes ago when you found the note. Did you—or do you—see anything else unusual or anyone near your home?"

"No." Kaylee had a good dead bolt, and Bear had a bark and a growl that would make anyone think twice, as long as they couldn't see him. However, when she glanced out the front window and into the darkness beyond, she couldn't help but shiver anyway.

"I'll ask Deputy Brooks to stop by on his patrol tonight," Nick said, "just to check the place out and check in on you."

"You really don't need to." As soon as Kaylee said the words she realized that she would feel better if he did send someone by.

"I'm going to anyway," Nick said firmly. "If someone is watching your property, they'll notice right away if a sheriff's deputy stops by and has a look around."

"All right. Thank you." She ended the call, then went to

make a cup of chamomile tea. She needed to relax, but she felt too keyed up at the moment to settle down. Maybe after Deputy Brooks investigated the area, she'd relax a little more.

Something deep down told her whoever had left the note was long gone. They were probably home, sleeping snug and warm on this winter's night. Or maybe they weren't. Clearly someone was nervous about Kaylee working for the sheriff's department. What if they were still out and about?

What were they so afraid she would find if she kept looking?

It wasn't long before Kaylee saw a pair of headlights in the darkness. They grew larger until she recognized a patrol car. The deputy left the car running and emerged with a flashlight. He took the steps to the door, where she met him.

"Good evening, ma'am. Deputy Alan Brooks," the young man said by way of introduction in a deep, booming voice. He was tall and muscular, and his head was shaved. His eyes were such a calm blue that Kaylee immediately relaxed. She vaguely remembered Aida mentioning that this was the youngest deputy in the department. "Deputy Durham sent me to have a look around. I'll let you know if I see anything or anyone, and I'll check back with you before I head out."

"Thank you very much." Kaylee shut the door, then sat down to wait. She imagined him rounding the house and shining his flashlight into the dormant fields of lavender out back. She could probably walk the property blindfolded herself. But tonight? No way. She was fine sitting here in the house letting someone else check things out. She registered a feeling of annoyance at not feeling safe in the house she'd known and loved from childhood.

Meanwhile, Bear paced from the front of the farmhouse to the back, as if conducting his own patrol.

She didn't doubt Bear would defend her if ever needed, but

he was such a little dog who saw a much bigger dog looking back at him in the mirror.

It seemed like only a few minutes before Deputy Brooks was lightly tapping on the door.

Kaylee went to answer it once again.

"All clear," Deputy Brooks announced. "Nothing seems out of place anywhere. I don't see anything that's been left behind other than that note."

"Thanks for checking. I feel better already."

"No problem. We Seattle transplants need to stick together," he told her with a wink.

"You're from Seattle too?" she asked.

He nodded. "I like it better here, though. People look out for each other."

"That they do," she agreed.

"May I have the note?" he asked. "I'll take it back to the station with me to put with the other one."

"Gladly." She surrendered it to him. "And thank you again."

Deputy Brooks nodded before walking down the steps and out to his patrol car.

Maybe it was nothing. Kaylee couldn't think that the person leaving the note would really harm her. Or would they? The real killer, she believed, was someone desperate and a bit rattled.

If someone was worried enough to threaten her, didn't that mean she was on the right track?

Or was it just some form of preemptive strike, and she wasn't even close to the truth?

12

The next morning, Kaylee woke up to find a light dusting of snow on the ground. It had fallen sometime during the night and gave a freshness to the world outside. Before Kaylee moved to Orcas Island she'd loved its summers, having spent several there with her grandparents while she was growing up. But now she was learning to love the island in all its seasons. So far she'd experienced fall, and now winter was on its way. Aside from the fact that a murderer was still unaccounted for, she found her new home a peaceful place.

"Come on, Bear," she called. "Let's go to work."

The dog dashed over to her, prancing in place while she fastened his leash. She knew that after years of leaving him at home when she went to work at the college, Bear looked forward to going to the shop with her just as much as she loved taking him along. Today he sported a bow tie in a festive green-and-red plaid.

After Kaylee brushed the snow from the windshield of the Escape, she settled them in the car and headed into the heart of downtown. Kaylee had already called ahead to The Sunfish Café to pick up a couple of breakfast croissant sandwiches for her and Mary. The café served light, tasty fare, and the locals were always good for a new story about something or someone in Turtle Cove. She wondered how many of those discussions were about the House of Christmas Trees and Kristopher Carroll that morning.

Kaylee left Bear in the vehicle while she went inside to pick up her order. As she walked through the door of the café, a bell jingled cheerfully above her head. The café was small, but the large windows made it feel less so. Booths in a tasteful aqua popped against the white floors under lights with coral shades. The counter was a sunny yellow that lent to the bright, open, modern feel. Kaylee loved this little café.

But she stopped dead in her tracks when she saw a couple having breakfast by the window.

Duncan and Sierra.

Sierra glanced up and noticed Kaylee. Then she focused on the coffee cup in front of her.

Instead of heading for the register, Kaylee made a beeline for their table. These were the last two people she expected to see dining together in such a relaxed setting.

"Good morning," Kaylee said. She knew she couldn't mask the astonishment that probably showed on her face, nor did she even try to.

"Hi, Kaylee." Sierra greeted her warmly. "Would you like to join us for breakfast?"

"No thank you. I'm just picking up an order to take with me to the shop." Kaylee stood there, feeling awkward and trying to figure out if there was a way to ask what they were doing together.

"Sierra's been telling me more about the island, and she said this little place was too good to pass up." Duncan smiled across the table at Sierra. "And she's right."

"Of course I'm right." Sierra gave Duncan a distinctly flirtatious grin.

Oh my. "Well, I should get going." Kaylee adjusted her purse strap on her shoulder. "Have a nice breakfast. I'll see you both very soon."

"See you soon," Sierra said, but she was looking at Duncan.

Kaylee's mind reeled as she headed for the register. Were Duncan and Sierra on a date? Was something brewing between the two of them? They seemed thick as thieves. She picked up the breakfast order, paid for it, and glanced at the two of them again when she left.

Kaylee and Bear drove to The Flower Patch. Mary hadn't arrived yet, so Kaylee turned up the heat, booted up the computers and the register, and switched on the lights in the workroom while Bear chose a spot to watch over the goings-on of the day.

The big tasks ahead of her were preparing table arrangements for delivery to Shaw Island for an afternoon holiday reception and preparing the ribbons for the arrangements that would grace the tables at tomorrow's memorial for Kris.

She shook her head as Duncan and Sierra popped into her mind again. Well, she wouldn't have pictured Barbara and Kris as a couple either. Maybe Duncan and Sierra had struck up a friendship, which was the most likely scenario. They'd all been through a lot, especially Sierra. Perhaps she liked Duncan's boyish banter and escapades, although others found the antics annoying. Maybe he helped Sierra forget her troubles for a while.

Kaylee mentally shrugged off the thoughts as she went to turn the sign on the front of the shop to *Open*. It was better not to speculate about others' personal lives, although it was a bit late for that. She wasn't the best source of wisdom when it came to relationships.

Yawning, she wondered if she had enough time to run next door for a cup of coffee from Jessica. Or should she just turn on the coffeepot in the office? Jessica would be the first to dish about the possibility of a new couple. She'd likely also concoct a possible murder theory related to the two of them.

In a scene reminiscent of a true crime show, Kaylee considered the idea of Duncan and Sierra working together to rid them both of a man who was strong competition for one and the long-lost father of the other. She scolded herself for letting her imagination run wild.

Then she came around to the obvious question again: Why

would Sierra murder Kris, her own father? What if she really harbored resentment for her mother struggling alone through Sierra's childhood while Sierra's father was becoming famous? Was that reason enough to kill him?

Yet Sierra's quiet and gentle demeanor made that idea less believable, even though her gun was the one that fired the bullet at Kris. When Sierra had dropped in at the Petal Pushers party, she'd seemed genuinely glad that she'd met her father and begun to build a relationship with him.

Kaylee jumped when the door opened.

"It's only me," Mary announced as she entered the shop. "I'm sorry I'm late. Herb hit the snooze button one too many times."

Kaylee yawned again. "I know the feeling. I was just thinking about running over to Jess's for coffee. Would you like one?"

"Yes, please."

"Oh, I brought croissant sandwiches from The Sunfish Café."

"That's great. I didn't have time to grab anything on my way out the door." Mary fished some bills from her wallet. "The coffee's on me today since you bought breakfast."

Kaylee accepted the bills with a smile. "Well, thank you. I'll be right back."

She headed next door to Death by Chocolate, bracing herself against a gust of wind.

When Kaylee entered the shop, she spotted a lone customer studying the goodies in a display case. The tall, fit man wore an Orcas Island sheriff's department uniform.

Kaylee came up next to Sheriff Eddie Maddox. "See anything good?"

Sheriff Maddox faced Kaylee and smiled, his dark brown eyes kind. He was in his late fifties, and his dark hair was peppered with gray. "I've been meaning to give you a wholehearted thank-you for your assistance on a particular case we've been working on lately."

"You're very welcome. I hope the information I've given you has been helpful."

"It certainly has," he said. "As a matter of fact, Mr. Akin has determined a cause of death, and we expect to make an arrest very soon."

"That's encouraging." Kaylee's mind whirled. What if they arrested Sierra?

"What a rotten time of year for this to happen." The sheriff shook his head. "Anytime is a bad time, of course, but I'm glad we'll get it wrapped up before Christmas."

Kaylee wanted to ask more details, but Jessica came out from the rear of the shop before she could do so.

"Thanks for waiting, Sheriff. When that timer goes off, I must answer it." Jessica pulled on a fresh pair of plastic serving gloves. "What can I get you this morning, sir?"

He rubbed his hands together. "Three pieces of chocolate. Surprise me. One for now, one for lunch, and one for coffee later. Susan says that's my limit. She'll know if I go past it."

"You've got it." Jessica glanced at Kaylee. "I'll be right with you, ma'am."

Kaylee rolled her eyes at her friend feigning such formality with her.

Sheriff Maddox eyed the éclairs. "I'm not sure if I've ever asked, but do you give out free samples?"

"I do occasionally. But wouldn't that count as one of your three pieces a day?" Jessica deposited three pieces of chocolate, one each of the fudge, a mini-brownie, and a petite cheesecake into a small square box.

"You're in league with my wife, aren't you?" the sheriff asked forlornly.

Jessica smiled at him.

"Sheriff Maddox, I'm curious about something," Kaylee said, stepping up to the counter. "I can ask you a case-related question, right?"

The sheriff took the box from Jessica, then turned to Kaylee. "You can ask, but I'm not sure if I can answer."

"Do you know of any type of relationship going on between Duncan McTavish and anyone here on the island?" Kaylee inquired, knowing that the sheriff was acquainted with just about everyone on Orcas Island.

"It depends on what kind of relationship you mean," Sheriff Maddox replied.

Kaylee took a deep breath and plunged ahead. "I was wondering if he's been romantically tied to anyone who is related to the current case you're working on."

Jessica raised her eyebrows. Kaylee knew she would have to do some explaining later.

Sheriff Maddox cocked his head. "I'm not aware of that."

"What about other kinds of relationships?" Kaylee persisted.

"Well, Mr. McTavish and Mr. Carroll were at odds in the past. They were competitors after all," the sheriff said. "We haven't really found anything that points a firm finger at him, though—not anything that would be a motive for murder. We know Mr. Carroll filed a suit against Mr. McTavish for defamation a few years ago, but nothing came of that."

"Is Duncan's alibi solid for the night Kris was killed?"

"Not rock solid, but what he told us about his whereabouts was verifiable."

Kaylee nodded. "Okay, thank you." She wasn't sure what she had expected to hear about Duncan, but if Sheriff Maddox was satisfied with the man's alibi, then she was too. Mostly.

"Any more questions?" he asked, giving her a sideways glance.

"Just one more. How did Mr. Carroll die?"

"I can't give you that answer yet. But I promise that all will be revealed in due time. Probably after the arrest." Sheriff Maddox's somber expression changed, and he smiled at her. "You talk to your grandma lately?" He had known Kaylee's grandparents for years.

"Yes. She loves Arizona. I don't think she's in a hurry for a visit north anytime soon." Kaylee laughed.

"This time of year, I don't blame her. Susan and I might join her in the warmer climate someday. Next time you talk to her, tell her hello for me."

"I most certainly will."

The sheriff paid for his order and thanked Jessica, then walked out.

As soon as the door closed behind him, Jessica pounced. "Who's seeing Duncan? And when did this happen?"

"I'm not positive about it. I probably shouldn't have brought it up." Kaylee scanned the menu. "Can I have two lattes?"

"Well, you did bring it up. So spill it." Jessica grinned as she stepped over to the coffee machine.

"This morning I stopped by The Sunfish Café to pick up croissant sandwiches, and I saw Duncan and Sierra having breakfast together."

"Huh. That doesn't necessarily have to mean anything."

"I know. But it was the *way* they were having breakfast. Almost like a couple."

"They weren't feeding each other, were they?"

Kaylee chuckled. "No, but I picked up on some flirting. I don't know how to explain it. Like they were concentrating on each other, and no one else in the place existed."

"That's interesting. Do you think anyone might have thought the same thing about you and Reese having dinner the other night?"

"Of course I did. But I definitely fed myself, and I did *not* flirt. It was just dinner, followed by the art show."

"Yes it was. Reese is a nice guy." Jessica glanced over Kaylee's shoulder before continuing. "I've had at least one person ask me if you two are an item."

"Oh goodness." Kaylee touched her cheeks, her hands feeling cool on her suddenly hot face. "I was worried someone might see us eating out."

"Relax. I don't think anyone seriously thinks that. It would have to be dinner twice, with lingering glances, for it to count in Turtle Cove."

"Oh dear. Well, I'm not in a hurry for that." Kaylee quickly changed the subject. "I'm glad the sheriff was willing to talk to us this morning, as much as he was able anyway. I wish I knew who they're planning to arrest and what the cause of death was, though."

"I bet the cause of death is something we're not expecting."

"You may be right."

Jessica finished preparing the lattes and poured them into paper cups with a flourish, then topped them with the lids. "There you go. I think some days I sell as much coffee as I do chocolates. Maybe more."

"Coffee and chocolate are a most excellent combination. I am so glad you sell both." Kaylee picked up the cups. "Off I go. Busy day ahead."

Jessica saluted her. "If I hear anything interesting, you'll be the first person I call."

Kaylee surveyed the floral garden taking up the rear of her

Escape. Two dozen table arrangements would soon make the short journey across the sound to Shaw Island.

There were many loyal customers of The Flower Patch who'd purchased from her grandmother for years and continued to do so from Kaylee. She aimed to work hard to keep their loyalty and business. The hotel on Shaw Island was a new customer, and they could have ordered their table displays from a number of florists. But the fact that they had chosen Kaylee's shop meant her business was growing. She felt a surge of pride.

"I'll be back later this afternoon," she told Mary before shutting the hatch on the Escape. The ferry ran several times a day between Orcas and Shaw, so Kaylee would have to wait a while before heading home to Orcas.

"Don't you worry. I'll have things covered on the home front," Mary reassured her.

Kaylee secured Bear in the passenger seat, and they took off.

Another thing Kaylee was proud of was her ability to negotiate the ferries like an island native. Besides locals traveling by boat on their own, ferries were a way of life on the San Juan Islands.

Kaylee was soon settled on the ferry, having parked her Escape and made her way up to the top, where she could watch their progress. The air had more bite to it in December, but the breathtaking view made up for the cold. She hoped to glimpse an orca breaching during this crossing. She'd seen them too many times to count, but it was always a treat.

Soon the waters of the sound flowed by the ferry. Bear was no doubt pouting below in her SUV, but he would get over it quickly. In a little while, Kaylee would rejoin him and wait for her turn to drive off the ferry. For now, she was content to watch the blue waters around her, take deep breaths of fresh air, and not think about the stressful or unpleasant events of the past week or so.

"You're the lady from the flower shop on Orcas." A woman

sitting across the aisle peered over the top of her paperback at Kaylee. "I remember you."

"Yes, I'm the owner of The Flower Patch. Where did I see you?"

"It was on television. You didn't see it?"

"See what?"

"It wasn't TV. Silly me, it was a video. Somewhere on the Internet. A bunch of animals stampeding in a mansion. The Turtle Cove Mansion on Orcas."

"I didn't know there was a video of that." *So much for not thinking about unpleasant things.* Kaylee made a mental note to look up the video online. "How did you find it?"

The woman chuckled. "My kids showed it to me. It sure was funny." Then she turned serious. "But then the same morning a guy was found dead at the mansion too. Now that's creepy if you ask me. You were right there when it happened, weren't you?"

Kaylee didn't know how to respond. "We definitely didn't expect it. So how did you know I was a florist?"

"Someone told me the lady who owned it retired, and her green-eyed granddaughter with a little dachshund bought the place."

"You're right again. That's me. And Bear."

"The guy narrating was telling about everyone on the video, and he was laughing about the animals."

"I guess it's a bit funny, looking back on it." A sick feeling crept into the pit of Kaylee's stomach. "Do you know who posted the video?"

"No. Search for 'Turtle Cove Mansion stampede.' It'll pop right up." The woman returned to her book.

Kaylee could scarcely wait to get back to Orcas, where she could take the time to satisfy her curiosity about the video. She wouldn't be surprised at all if Duncan was behind the video too. Was his comical manner a cover-up for something darker? For Sierra's sake, Kaylee hoped not. What did Sierra see in an immature guy like Duncan?

Kaylee's brain was in overdrive. She made the delivery to her customer and headed back to the ferry on autopilot, her mind spinning with possibilities.

When Kaylee and Bear returned to The Flower Patch, she held down the fort while Mary took a lunch break and ran some errands. Mary had already tucked the ribbons for Kaylee's mansion project into one basket, along with boxes of picks, floral wire, wire cutters, needle-nose pliers, and other tools she would need to create the arrangements.

She sent Jessica a text: *Plans for dinner? We need to look at social media.*

About five minutes later, Jessica replied: *Come to my place. We're having pizza—nothing fancy but that means less cleanup. And bring Bear!*

By the time the shop closed for the day, Kaylee wanted nothing more than to go home and soak in the tub with some lavender bath salts. Instead, she packed Bear into the Escape and drove to Jessica's house.

Jessica greeted her at the door. "Come on in. Luke is watching a game, and all I had planned was a night with a mystery novel. I'd rather work on our own real-life mystery instead. Who knows what we'll find?"

Kaylee let Bear scamper into the house ahead of her. He'd been to Jessica's before and knew his way around. "Maybe nothing. But there's something I need to show you before we dive into our investigation."

Bear had tangled himself up in his leash, which he'd wrapped around himself twice. He looked at them for help.

Jessica squatted down beside him and freed him. "Bear, you're awfully excited to be here. Did you get left behind today?" She glanced up at Kaylee.

"Only on the ferry ride to Shaw. I couldn't avoid it. That's why I promised him an evening out."

"I made him a special doggy pizza." Jessica motioned for Kaylee to follow her into the kitchen. Already the roar of a football game came from the den. "Must be time for the kickoff."

"Doggy pizza?"

"Yes, it has a 'sauce' of peanut butter, with treats and lean cooked chicken on top." Jessica grabbed a paper plate from the counter. "Voilà!"

Bear's pointy nose twitched, and he started to dance on the kitchen tile.

"Here you go, my little friend." Jessica set the plate on the floor in the corner.

Bear scurried over to his dinner and began eating.

"You're going to spoil him," Kaylee said, as if she didn't do plenty of that herself.

Jessica waved a hand dismissively. "The pizza's here," she announced, "so help yourself and let's dig in."

Two pizza boxes rested on the counter, and Kaylee caught a whiff of pepperoni. Her stomach growled. She put two slices of pizza on a plate, then settled down next to Jessica at the breakfast bar. She had made sure her phone was fully charged before she left the shop. She didn't want Jessica to miss the video.

"Well," Jessica said around a bite of pizza, "I have to say, we should have probably had some salad with this. I didn't set it out, but I have some in the fridge."

"First we need to watch this video. A woman on the ferry told me about it, and I've been dying of curiosity ever since." Kaylee pulled up the search engine and found the video.

The animals burst through the doorway of the mansion. The

phone's image bobbed, as if whoever held it was chasing the goat as it hurtled through the entry. Kaylee then heard herself shouting over the goat's bleating. The goat flashed by the camera as it dragged the ribbon across the hall and into the parlor. Barbara shrieked.

"Please tell me you're not filming this," they heard Mary say.

"Uh no, ma'am." a television reporter responded.

The image shifted to Duncan. He leaned on the end of the stair's railing, laughing. He waved at the camera. "Dude, you made it. Sweet."

Now the camera focused on Kaylee, pounding up the stairs. She waved at the geese and said something to Barbara below. Did her voice always sound so shrill? But she was in shock and she was stressed at that moment, so maybe not.

After almost three minutes of video played out, Jessica commented, "That was something else. Who recorded it?"

"I'm not sure. Maybe a reporter." Kaylee glanced at the phone. "Did you notice the floor? There were streaks leading from the rear hallway to the closet. The floor's shiny, so the only way you can see them is in the reflection. It didn't get muddy until the goat and the big birds ran through."

"Very interesting."

Kaylee nodded. "I'm forwarding a link to the video to Nick."

"I'm sure that's helpful. Those streaks could be a major clue."

"I think so too."

Jessica's phone began to chime.

She hopped from the barstool, snatched up her phone, and checked the number. "He came through!" She answered the call before Kaylee could ask what she was talking about. "This is Jessica . . . Great! . . . No, we don't mind coming in." Jessica glanced at Kaylee. "We'll be there in a few minutes. Do you mind if we bring a dog with us? . . . Okay, thanks."

As soon as the call ended, Kaylee asked, "What was that all

about?"

"Marvin Jones, the freelance photographer who took photos for the newspaper at the reception, is sharing them with us. He's at his home office now and has the photos laid out for us to see. We can bring Bear too."

At that, Bear wagged his tail excitedly.

Kaylee grinned. "I'm intrigued. Let's go."

They piled into Kaylee's Escape, with Bear seeming a bit disappointed that he had been relegated to the backseat. Jessica directed Kaylee to a quaint residential neighborhood not far from downtown. They pulled up in front of a house with a detached garage. A sign read *Jones Photography*.

Marvin Jones met them at the door. He was an older man, slightly balding, with a voice that reminded Kaylee of Winnie the Pooh. "Good evening, ladies." He looked at Bear. "And who is this handsome fellow?"

"This is Bear." Kaylee extended her hand. "And I'm Kaylee Bleu."

"Nice to meet you." He shook her hand, then ushered them inside and motioned to a nearby table. "I made two sets of prints of the reception. The sheriff's department already has one set. This is the other."

Jessica headed for the table. She pulled a notebook from her purse.

Marvin stood between the two of them. "Every photo has source information in the image properties section of the data file. So I've arranged these in the order I took them during the evening."

Kaylee nodded. "Good."

Marvin pointed to the top left photo. "This one was taken first. It was shortly after everyone arrived. They're laid out in chronological order from there."

"That's perfect. Thank you," Kaylee said.

"No problem. You ladies take as much time as you like with the photos. If you have any questions, I'll be editing pictures at my desk."

Jessica jotted something down in her notebook.

Kaylee glanced at the notebook and realized that it was a list of everyone at the reception.

Jessica pointed at a photo of Kris and Meghan posing for the camera. "This time stamp says eight thirty, so it was taken around the time Kris told Meghan he wasn't feeling well. He left soon after this, I think."

Kaylee had learned that Duncan and Meghan were the last to leave, with Sierra locking the door behind all three of them because she had the key to the mansion. No one was quite sure when Barbara left. "I remember talking with Barbara. She kept yawning, saying her sleeping pill was kicking in."

"I'll put a question mark by Barbara's name," Jessica said.

Kaylee studied the list, which Jessica had embellished with notes. "I don't see anything in these photos. No negative interactions. Just the timeline. It doesn't really matter when we left. What matters is what happened after we left."

"Exactly." Jessica underlined all the names.

Bear sighed from where he lay under the table by Kaylee's feet.

"I know, Bear." Kaylee had to smile. Then she looked across the room to where Marvin sat at a computer. "Mr. Jones, you took a lot of pictures, but what if you missed someone?"

"I took a small group photo around nine. It was one of the last pictures I took. Everyone still at the mansion was in that photo." Marvin rose from his desk chair and rejoined them at the table. "Here it is." He tapped a photo in the bottom row of pictures.

Kaylee scanned the faces. There she was, along with Mary, Barbara, Duncan, Meghan, and Sierra. "It looks like Kris is the only one missing."

So how did he end up in that closet?

13

Barbara entered The Flower Patch on Wednesday, bringing a blast of cold air right along with her. It looked like she'd been crying.

Kaylee was stocking fresh inventory while Bear snored underneath the coffee table in the consultation area. She had arrived at the shop early and was all set to knock out two days' worth of work in one. She knew she'd lose some time on Thursday along with part of the day Friday in preparing for the House of Christmas Trees. She didn't want to make a habit of leaning on Mary as much as she had been lately.

"The reason I'm here is to confirm the flower arrangements for the memorial this afternoon." Barbara wiped her eyes. "I'm sorry. It's hitting me again today. I just can't believe this—this all has happened."

Kaylee nodded. "It's been an incredible shock." She wouldn't forget the moment Meghan opened that closet door at the mansion anytime soon.

"Anyway, I'm doing what I must, seeing to business. I know it's what Kris would have wanted. So what is the status of my order?"

Kaylee walked over to the counter and pulled up Barbara's order on the computer. "It's next in line upstairs, and I'm almost ready to assemble the arrangements. I have two Winter's Splendor arrangements that will be displayed on pillars beside the podium. I have a Christmas Elegance ready for the food table and Holiday Spirit next to the coffeepot."

Barbara joined her at the counter. "May I see the designs

again? I want to make sure they're perfect. I've been in such a fog these days that I'm not even sure what I ordered."

"Of course." Kaylee ran upstairs to the office to fetch the design book. Pictures of the designs she offered came in handy for customers who weren't sure what to order. Kaylee considered the book a treasure and would keep it always.

Barbara had pored over the design book with Mary the other day. Not only was Barbara unsure, but in the end Mary said Barbara selected the original arrangements she'd vacillated over in the first go-round. After that little session, Mary had gone home with a migraine.

When Kaylee returned, she offered Barbara a chair in the consultation area, and they both sat down.

"Here's what you've selected." Kaylee opened the book to the Christmas arrangements section. "Like I said, I'm almost ready to put together the arrangements, so now is a good time for any last-minute changes."

"Then my timing is ideal," Barbara said, skimming the page.

"That it is." Kaylee glanced at Bear, who still snored under the coffee table. *Lucky dog.*

The bell over the door jangled again, and Aida Friedman strolled in.

Kaylee smiled and greeted her.

"Where's that little buddy of yours?" Aida asked as she scanned the sales floor.

"Bear's over here, sawing logs." Kaylee motioned to the coffee table. "Are you here for your usual? I'll be able to help you in a few minutes."

"Yes, but take your time. I'll go inhale some of those soap scents." Aida made her way over to the display of DeeDee's handmade soaps.

Kaylee turned her attention back to Barbara, who muttered

to herself as she leafed through the book.

"Oh, go right ahead. Please help your friend." Barbara looked up from the book. "I'll be a few minutes."

That didn't bode well. But then, she'd just told Barbara that now would be a good time to make any changes for the memorial flowers. She hoped she had whatever Barbara wanted to change in stock.

Kaylee went over to the refrigerator case to assist Aida.

"You don't have to help me this time if you're busy," Aida said, glancing at Barbara. "I know where all the carnations are."

"Of course I don't mind helping you. Not in the least." Maybe if she waited long enough, Barbara would realize the flower arrangements she'd already chosen were perfectly fine for the event.

Aida picked out three *Dianthus caryophyllus* of each color. "I don't know what it is about carnations, but they always make me smile. I think it's because they remind me of bright, fun little pom-poms."

"I can agree with that." Kaylee slipped the flowers into a plastic, cone-shaped sleeve, then headed for the register to key in Aida's purchase. "Will there be anything else for you today?"

"Not today, but I'll be back next week as usual. I might pick up a few last-minute gifts before I visit my boyfriend over Christmas. I'd like to get something for his family that will be easy to transport."

"I'm sure we'll find something," Kaylee said, "even if it's not floral."

"Thanks." Aida gave her a wide smile. "I'll see you later." She glanced toward Barbara, who was still studying the design book as if the fate of nations rested upon her floral arrangement decisions, then leaned over the counter and lowered her voice. "I'm not sure if you've heard the news, but—"

"She's been arrested!" Jessica burst into The Flower Patch, carrying two covered cups of coffee. The bang of the door drowned out the jingle of the bells and roused Bear from his nap.

"Who?"

"Sierra," Jessica blurted out.

Mary emerged from the staircase that led to the office upstairs. "What? Why?" She glanced at Kaylee. "Did you know this was going to happen?"

"No," Kaylee said honestly. "Sheriff Maddox told me yesterday that they were close to making an arrest. But I didn't think it would be this soon, and he didn't tell me who it would be." She handed Aida her carnations. "As always, thank you."

Aida held up her carnations. "No, thank *you*." Then she scurried from the shop.

No one said anything else until the door was firmly shut behind her.

"Here. I thought you two might need a pick-me-up." Jessica gave Kaylee and Mary the coffee she'd brought in. "It's all over the news this morning. KSEA even had it on the Seattle morning show."

"What did they have on Sierra to arrest her?" Kaylee wondered aloud.

"Apparently, Kristopher Carroll took out a $500,000 life insurance policy this fall, and he named Sierra the sole beneficiary," Jessica explained.

Kaylee shook her head. "Which means Sierra went from having no reason to benefit from Kris's death to five hundred thousand reasons. I hope she called an attorney."

"She promised us she would." Mary took a sip of coffee.

Barbara rose from her chair. "I can't believe they've made an arrest already." Her cheeks were flushed. She blew her nose, then tossed the tissue in the trash can. "And Sierra, his own *daughter*.

Or that's what they said. I don't know if it's really the truth."

"If she killed him?" Kaylee asked.

Barbara gave Kaylee a sharp glance. "No, if she's his daughter. Kris never mentioned seeing a birth certificate. He also never mentioned taking a paternity test so he could prove it one way or the other. And he would have told me, you know? It all seems very fishy to me."

"So did you know all along that Kris believed he was Sierra's father?" Jessica asked.

"This summer, not long after we met, Kris said he'd had a fling years and years ago with a woman who lived on the island. A summertime thing. He told me he believed he might have a daughter, but he wasn't sure how to go about finding her. After that, he dropped it. Never talked about it again."

"Did he ever tell you a name?" Kaylee asked.

"He couldn't remember." Barbara sighed. "I was beginning to become a bit concerned about his memory. He'd forget things here and there. I figured it was just the artist in him. We can be forgetful sometimes in spite of our genius."

Kaylee ventured another question. "Why do you think Sierra would kill him if she believed he was her father?"

"You'd have to ask her." Barbara's eyes glittered with unshed tears, and she dashed them away. "But I think it was greed. She just wanted some money and knew my beloved Kristopher was the cash cow who'd bring it to her."

"What about a will?" Jessica asked. "If there was life insurance, surely there was a will."

"It hasn't been read yet because the investigation was ongoing. Regardless, I wasn't advised about it." Barbara inhaled sharply. "Kris and I had talked about what to do with our belongings, our legacies. We both agreed we would change our wills now that we had each other."

Kaylee pondered that. If Kris had been planning to change his will, then Barbara would have likely benefited from it. But $500,000? Sierra wouldn't be rolling in money, but she would certainly be comfortable. It was definitely a plausible motive. But the idea that Sierra could do something like that made Kaylee's stomach turn. She had befriended Sierra, and she didn't want to think such horrible thoughts about her.

The shop door burst open again, banging into the wall behind it. Duncan stormed inside. "Ladies, Sierra's been—" He stopped and glared at Barbara.

The older woman returned his glare. "Whatever you have to say, say it, Mr. McTavish. You should be grateful that fingers aren't pointing at you."

"You had something to do with Sierra's arrest." Duncan motioned to Barbara. "You never liked that Sierra was Kris's daughter and that he paid attention to her. You didn't want to share him with anyone."

Barbara shook her head. "I don't know what you mean by sharing. I was bracing myself to share Kris with the world because of his show. Anyway, I always suspected Sierra's motives for suddenly wanting to get to know him, and now my suspicions have been confirmed."

"Let's try to calm down," Kaylee said. "I'm not happy that Sierra's been arrested either."

"It's a mistake," Duncan said. "They've got the wrong person. I know it."

"And how, pray tell, do you know?" Barbara asked icily.

"I just do." Duncan glanced at each of them in turn.

"You sound awfully guilty to me." Barbara narrowed her eyes. "Did you help her?"

"Of course I didn't help her," Duncan snapped. "She didn't do it!"

Mary stepped in. "Please, Barbara. You're upset about Kris, and I don't blame you. Today you have the chance to remember him, and I know it's going to be a beautiful memorial."

Barbara's features softened. "You're right. It will be." She took a deep breath and exhaled. Then she looked at Duncan and scowled again. "If I don't see you at the memorial I won't mind. At all."

Duncan snorted. "Just try to keep me away." He stomped from the shop as abruptly as he'd arrived.

This memorial will be nothing if not interesting.

14

On Wednesday afternoon Kristopher Carroll's friends and acquaintances gathered at Death by Chocolate for his memorial. Jessica had enlisted the Petals' help to pull off the feat of transforming her shop into a reception space. They had moved all the tables along one wall and set up the chairs in rows.

Someone had put up a screen on an open wall, where a projector displayed a video of Kris throughout the years.

Barbara—clad in black from her boots to her wide-brimmed hat, except for a strand of white pearls around her neck—was in her element, greeting everyone who walked through the door and indicating empty seats. It was clear she would run the show.

Kaylee leaned against the counter and perused the program Barbara presented to all who entered the shop.

Memorial for Kristopher Carroll

Welcome—Barbara Lang-Masters

Eulogy—Barbara Lang-Masters

Memories—All

Special video presentation—Barbara Lang-Masters

Please sign the guest book and include your favorite memory of Kristopher Carroll, our designer Santa.

All she could do was blink after she read the whole thing.

Duncan accepted a program from Barbara, who regarded him as if he were a cockroach and she was debating about getting a can of spray. But she said nothing as he refused the offer of a seat and instead stood in a corner of the room.

His typical I'm-here-for-the-party demeanor had been ramped down a few notches this afternoon. He wore a charcoal-gray sport coat over a lighter gray button-down shirt, with black trousers and loafers.

His eyes locked with Kaylee's, and he nodded at her.

Kaylee stepped away from the counter to cross the room to talk to him, but it looked like Barbara was ready to begin the memorial. Kaylee kept her spot at the counter, within earshot in case Jessica needed help with the chocolate soufflés now baking in the oven.

"Thank you all for coming today." Barbara managed a smile. "When I met Kristopher in August of this year, I knew he would change my life. I never imagined, though, that I would be standing here today, speaking to honor his life."

Barbara picked up a handkerchief and dabbed at her eyes. "I'm sorry. I didn't think it would be this difficult." She paused, clearing her throat.

She then read a brief obituary, outlining the details of Kris's life, his early years, the discovery of his talent, and the impact he'd had on thousands of people. "Even here in Turtle Cove, Kristopher wanted to make a difference in people's lives, both now and in the future, by investing in Orcas Island students who might not have been able to further their education otherwise."

Barbara didn't mention his summers at the island or his daughter, Sierra Underwood. She had edited her take on Kristopher Carroll's story and portrayed herself as the star of the show for the last months of his life.

"So we remember him now. We will never forget the man who stole our hearts, made us smile, made us laugh, and could have done so much more." Barbara bowed her head for a moment, then looked up.

Should we applaud? Kaylee glanced toward the kitchen. Maybe Jessica needed help after all. She started to clap, and a few followed suit, including Reese, the rest of the Petals and their spouses, and other members of the House of Christmas Trees committee. Meghan clapped twice, then wiped her eyes. Duncan didn't clap. Nor did Sheriff Maddox, but he did nod at Kaylee, and she nodded back.

Barbara continued. "Now I invite you to watch a never-before-seen video that I was able to obtain a copy of. It's the pilot episode of *Celebrate with Kris.*"

Someone dimmed the lights as Barbara pushed a button on a nearby laptop and the video started playing on the screen.

A pan—or something else metal—clattered in the kitchen. Jessica's mutter could be heard at the counter.

That was Kaylee's cue. She headed for the kitchen.

With her hands on her hips, Jessica stared at an upside-down tray of soufflés on the kitchen floor. "Well, if this isn't just a fine batch of chocolate!"

"Oh no," Kaylee said.

"Barbara had me cook and prepare for fifty, and there's twenty-five people here, tops." Jessica snatched up a pair of pot holders and lifted the sheet pan off the soufflés. They made round, brown splotches on the tile floor. "What a waste of time and ingredients. And this lovely chocolate."

"You keep plating whatever you need to. I'll get this cleaned up." Kaylee grabbed a roll of paper towels and began picking up the sad little soufflés. "I bet they would have tasted delicious."

"Oh, it's small consolation, but, yes, they would have been

magnificent." Jessica wiped her forehead with the back of one hand. "Now I need to wash my hands. Again."

Kaylee managed to get the worst of the mess cleaned up, then found a mop in the cleaning closet along with some tile cleaner. She made quick work of the smears of chocolate on the floor.

Meanwhile, Jessica finished plating the remainder of the desserts. "Thank you. Now I can get these set out, so all the refreshments will be available immediately after the show finishes. *Immediately.*"

"Don't let me stop you." Kaylee shooed her away. "Go." She gave a soft chuckle despite the seriousness of the event.

When Jessica had slipped from the room, she looked around. She didn't see anything else that needed tending to, no more imminent disasters either—excluding Oliver the limp geranium. Kaylee entered the sales floor of the shop, where Kris filled the screen.

He was talking about the ongoing transformation of two children's bedrooms into whimsical places to sleep, play, and study. The home for the project in this episode, Kris said, was owned by a single mother who'd recently lost her job. She didn't know it yet, but the children's room makeover was paid for—along with six months of mortgage payments until she got back on her feet.

"That's what it's all about," he told the individual who was his assistant on the show. "We're taking these spaces and freshening them up and organizing them. When you've hit rock bottom, you don't think about extras like this. You're just trying to get the bills paid. We want to help people thrive, give them the small niceties they can't give themselves."

The episode concluded with a reveal to the mother and her son and daughter. One would need to have a heart of stone not to feel a surge of emotion when Kris told the mother—a woman whose obvious exhaustion made her look about ten years older than she was—that her house payment was also covered for the next six months.

She gave a happy sob and buried her face on Kris's shoulder.

He patted her back, smiling. "Life's about a celebration, and I want you to have some reasons to celebrate," he said.

The show ended, this time with far more genuine applause coming from the group assembled in the shop, without prompting from Kaylee or anyone else. She clapped too. *He wasn't doing it to make himself look good. He didn't ham it up for the camera. He was totally focused on making this woman's life better.*

Kris's show would have been spectacular if this pilot episode was any indication.

Barbara switched on the main lights. "Kris was a remarkable man, as I'm sure you can tell. Thank you all for coming. And now, Mrs. Jessica Roberts is presenting the best of her shop's refreshments for all of us. Please enjoy."

Duncan glanced Kaylee's way again. He beckoned to her, then slipped outside.

She nodded and followed him out the front door, shivering as she did so. She'd left her coat in Jessica's office.

"What is it?" Kaylee said, rubbing her arms to warm them up.

With the door closed behind them, Duncan glanced over her shoulder. "Sierra's arrest stinks of a setup. It's too convenient. I tried to call her, but they wouldn't let me talk to her. She's lawyered up, which is good, but I'm still worried. Oh, and by the way, I'm sorry about earlier today."

The door opened, and Sheriff Maddox walked out. He greeted Kaylee and gave Duncan a nod. "Mr. McTavish, I presume."

"You presume right, sir—uh, Sheriff," Duncan said. He shuffled his feet, clearly uncomfortable around the lawman.

"Don't stand outside here talking too long, you two." Sheriff

Maddox sounded nonchalant. "It's cold, and that chocolate in there is disappearing at an alarming rate."

"We'll go back in soon." Kaylee watched him head to his car. Why was Sheriff Maddox here? He had a penchant for all things chocolate, especially anything Jessica sold. But if they had someone in custody already, why did he still seem to be searching? Kaylee had the distinct impression that the sheriff didn't think his case was wrapped up.

"He's still looking for suspects. He has to be. Even though they've already arrested someone," Duncan said, as if he knew what Kaylee was thinking. "Which is why I'm talking to you. You need to call Bentley Design in Portland, Oregon. Ask for Estelle Bentley and tell her I gave you her name. Check with her about Meghan Benson and the portfolio she submitted with her résumé." He handed her a folded slip of paper.

Kaylee studied it. "Why are you telling me this instead of Sheriff Maddox? You can probably catch up with him if you go now."

"Because I know he'd wonder if I'm trying to throw suspicion off myself by putting it on Meghan."

"Are you?" Kaylee asked.

Duncan sighed. "Come on. We talked about this before. I admit to being jealous of Kris's success. Even from the grave—not that he's in it yet—he's showing people up, including me. But being jealous doesn't mean I'd do something to hurt the guy. Just like I don't think Sierra killed her father for five hundred grand. But here's the thing . . . I don't have a squeaky-clean record. It wouldn't take much for the police to turn their attention to me, so I'm trying to lie low as much as possible."

"What did you do?"

"Back in college I was in jail for six months for assault. It's embarrassing to admit now. I destroyed another student's work for a competition because I wanted to win. He tried to grab it from me, so I shoved him and he hit his head on the doorframe. It's been more than ten years, but I consider myself lucky to have a career at all."

Kaylee nodded, but she wasn't sure she trusted this man. As a matter of fact, she was sure she didn't trust him. "True, that was a long time ago. Like I said, though, why are you telling me this now? Why didn't you tell the police?"

"I'm sure they know. Like I said, I don't want to draw any more attention to myself than I've already had with all this. Negative attention, that is, with my show getting ready to film."

Kaylee was sure her nose was frozen. She wanted to go back inside, so she quickly considered everything he said and his request. "All right, I'll call Ms. Bentley."

"I just don't want any more questions asked of me," Duncan said. "If the sheriff wants to know why you called the design firm, you can tell him it was because of me."

"Fair enough."

"Estelle should give you some very interesting information." Duncan stepped onto the sidewalk. "See you tomorrow to set up at the mansion."

"See you." Yes, tomorrow was the big day.

Kaylee hurried back inside the shop, shivering. She might as well have a chocolate scone and a cup of hot tea. After all, wasn't that why they were gathered here? To remember Kris and help Barbara through her grief? With all the woman's histrionics, it seemed like Barbara really did love him. Or she loved the attention she was getting because of him. Kaylee scolded herself for the uncharitable thought.

Inside, people in groups of two or three visited in hushed tones. DeeDee and Mary talked to a woman who looked a lot like Barbara. That must be Barbara's sister, Bernice, whom

Barbara had supposedly left the house to avoid the other day.

Barbara sat in the corner as she sipped from a cup and nibbled on a cookie. She set the cup on a nearby table, then stared down at her plate. All her animation was gone.

"She's devastated in more ways than one, I'm afraid," Bernice said. "Please keep an eye on her while the group is decorating. I don't know what she'll do."

A parcel deliveryman entered Death by Chocolate. He held a shipping envelope.

Jessica approached him. "A delivery?"

"Yes, but it's not for you." He scanned the crowd. "Is Barbara Lang-Masters here? A neighbor said she'd be here today."

"I'm Barbara Lang-Masters." Barbara rose and crossed the floor of the shop. She took the offered envelope. As she did, her face brightened. "Oh, I've been waiting for this."

Barbara signed for the envelope, and as the deliveryman headed out the door, she ripped open the edge and pulled out some folded sheets of paper. "They're from the lawyer," she told Bernice excitedly.

Kaylee watched as Barbara unfolded the document. Whatever it was, Barbara almost looked as if she were ready to smile.

Barbara's face went from an expression of expectancy to almost delight, then fell again. Her brow furrowed. She tossed the papers on the floor.

"He left me out of his will. After promising he would include me."

On Wednesday evening, the workroom at The Flower Patch practically burst with evergreen garland, blue roses and magnolias, glass ornaments in three sizes and multiple shades of blue and gray, with silver ornaments on the side. And foam. Plenty of floral foam.

Kaylee, Mary, and Reese could hardly squeeze through the space. More supplies for the other designers' work had taken over a great deal of the shop's main showroom. Meghan was due to pick up her supplies for Kris's design first thing on Thursday morning.

Barbara, who still insisted her design was a big secret, had declined to order anything through Kaylee's supplier, which was fine with Kaylee.

Duncan's floral and plant order was ready for pickup as well. He'd already told Kaylee he would also be by first thing Thursday morning to tote everything over to the mansion. Which, in Duncan time, likely meant he'd arrive by eleven thirty or noon on Thursday, in which case Mary would be there taking care of the shop and could help him.

"There's no way we can get any prep work started here tonight," Kaylee told her two friends who stood across the expanse of poinsettias and other bright red flowers. "There's simply no room to do anything."

Bear wound his way between boxes and buckets, his nose in the air. Then he sneezed.

"You look exhausted," Mary said to Kaylee. "Go home and get a good night's sleep. Come back in the morning, and we'll get you loaded up and over to the mansion."

Kaylee nodded. "I'm not going to argue with you on this one."

"What about the trees at the mansion? Have they been set up yet?" Reese asked.

"I insisted that we go with artificial trees for the taller displays, so there will be far less mess when they're transported after the open house." Kaylee checked her list. "We've already set up a blue spruce and a noble fir along with a few other trees in the mansion. Barbara coordinated it."

"Unbelievable." Mary shook her head. "Evidently Sierra was right when she made the comment last week that Barbara would like nothing more than to take over the committee."

"If everything unfolds like it should at the open house," Kaylee said, "I don't care who runs the show as long as I don't have to. I don't have time. And neither do you, I'm sure."

"I hate to say this about anyone," Mary went on, "but Barbara has such an intolerable manner sometimes. I'm glad I'll be here manning the store."

"Lucky you," Kaylee agreed. "Though I did feel a bit sorry for her today when she learned that Kris didn't include her in his will."

"I wonder who he *did* include in his will. Sierra, maybe?" Mary asked.

"I have no idea." Kaylee remembered an earlier conversation when Sierra admitted that she didn't even know if Kris had a will.

Reese yawned. "Ladies, it's been a busy day, and tomorrow will be even busier. And so, I bid you both good night."

"Thank you for your help," Kaylee said. "Both in the past and in advance. I'll see you in the morning."

But before she saw them both the following morning, she had an important phone call to make.

15

Kaylee stood in the kitchen at Wildflower Cottage on Thursday morning. She held the slip of paper that Duncan had given to her yesterday at Kris's memorial.

A receptionist at the design firm put her straight through to Estelle Bentley. Kaylee hadn't thought about how she'd explain the reason for her call.

"This is Estelle." The timbre of the woman's voice reminded Kaylee of a Hollywood starlet from days gone by.

"Good morning. My name is Kaylee Bleu. I'm the owner of The Flower Patch in Turtle Cove, Washington. I was given your number by Mr. Duncan McTavish."

"Oh, Duncan, of course. What a charming young man, although a bit of a rapscallion. How is he? Have you seen him recently?"

"As a matter of fact, I have. We're working together on a project here on Orcas Island—"

"What a delightful place!" she exclaimed. "In the San Juan Islands, correct?"

"That's right. The project is the House of Christmas Trees, a fund-raiser for scholarships here on the island. Anyway, he gave me your number—"

"I'd love to donate something," Estelle interrupted again, "but this isn't a good time of year for us, dear."

Kaylee chuckled. "I'm not seeking a donation. What I'm looking for is some information."

"How intriguing," Estelle purred. "I certainly hope I can help you."

"I'm curious to know what dealings you've had with a designer by the name of Meghan Benson—"

"A conniving snip. Just hearing her name puts my teeth on edge. Let me tell you this. Four weeks ago—I've got the date on my calendar—I invited her to an interview at our design offices here in Portland. We have a junior lead designer position I thought she'd be perfect for. At the time."

"At the time?" Kaylee asked, shocked that she'd managed to get all the words out.

"That's right. She showed me a stunning portfolio. Fresh and innovative. I could tell she'd interned and worked for Kristopher Carroll. Of course I knew she worked for him. It was on her résumé. But her designs proved it. Well, I do a little checking. After talking with Kristopher himself, I find out that she swiped his designs and tried to pass them off as her own! Did you ever?"

"Oh, that's terr—"

"Yes, it's tantamount to a crime. When I informed Kristopher what she'd shown me as her own work, he was livid. He told me he'd deal with her straightaway. It's intellectual property, and I take disclosure of company secrets and proprietary information very seriously here."

"I understand that compl—"

"If she has applied to work for your company, I strongly encourage you to reconsider. Or at the very least, do not allow her anywhere near your company secrets or proprietary information, if you have any."

"That's very interesting. No, I'm not planning to hire—"

"Does this have anything to do with Mr. Carroll's death, by any chance? I heard he passed recently. You would think that the authorities would want to speak with me. Never mind. You know what? I'll call them. They need to know about that poisonous little thief. Whom should I speak with on Turtle Island?"

"Orcas Island. You should call the sheriff's department in Eastsound and ask for Deputy Nick Durham. He's in charge of the investigation."

"Investigation?" Estelle shrilled. "Goodness, that's even more intriguing."

"Thank you for your time, Ms. Bentley."

"Anytime, Ms. Green."

Kaylee was about to remind Estelle that her last name was Bleu, not Green, but the woman had already hung up. *Okay, then.* Kaylee stared at the phone, breathless. She'd never had a conversation with someone so intent on answering her own questions.

Well, Meghan Benson, what have you really been up to?

She drank another cup of coffee as she planned her day. She needed to stop at The Flower Patch to prepare the flowers and greenery, load everything in her vehicle, and drive to the mansion and set up the arrangements.

"Are you ready to go to the shop?" she asked Bear, who sat by her feet.

The dog sighed, then rested his long snout on his paws and looked up at her with his big eyes.

"I know. It'll be a long day, and you'll be at the shop while I'm out and about." She wished she could bring Bear with her to the mansion, but the owner was adamant that no dogs or animals of any kind be allowed in the house, especially since the prank.

Kaylee hoped the other unpleasantness at the mansion also wouldn't be repeated.

Reese's truck was parked at The Flower Patch when Kaylee

arrived. *Good.* She'd already assembled the tools she'd need and put them in a tool kit, which she normally used when setting up floral arrangements that had to be assembled on-site at an event.

Once inside, Kaylee saw that Mary, efficient as always, had gathered the components for each section of the display into their own separate areas, with Kaylee's design notebook containing the sketches on the counter next to the tool kit.

Bear made a beeline for the nearest containers of blooms and gave them intensely investigative sniffs. Then he noticed Reese standing nearby and trotted over to him, with a big doggy smile.

Reese petted the dog, then turned to Kaylee. "Good morning. It looks like Mary has everything ready for us to load up."

"I would be so lost without her," Kaylee confessed.

Mary emerged from the office area. "You're Bea's grand-daughter. You'd manage. I got here around seven. Even in the morning light, it was still a bit overwhelming, so I've put Duncan's stuff over there." She nodded in the direction of the seating area for consultations.

Kaylee took in Duncan's outlandish order. It looked as if a jungle had overgrown the furniture. She could scarcely make out the love seat and matching ottoman, along with the coffee table nearby.

"Tropical plants *and* evergreens?" Kaylee wondered how in the world she hadn't noticed them in the order. Of course she had. She just hadn't thought much about it at the time. Now, though, it looked like Christmas was doing battle with a luau. Even Bear stared at them as if they didn't make sense.

"Meghan picked up her order, and she's on her way to the mansion," Mary said.

"I guess we'd better do the same." Kaylee glanced at Reese. "I've already stopped by Death by Chocolate for some cream-filled éclairs. For a little motivation."

"I'm feeling incredibly motivated just by the sound of that." Reese stepped over to a crate containing four poinsettia plants and hefted it. "We'll get this loaded in no time."

In reality it took them nearly thirty minutes to get everything loaded into her SUV and his truck, then a good ten minutes for Kaylee to make sure nothing would tip over on the ride through town.

Before they set off, Kaylee said good-bye to Bear, who was curled up in his bed. The little dog was already worn-out from running back and forth to and from the vehicles and trying to figure out what the humans were doing.

The mansion was a bustle of activity when they pulled up in front of the grand home. Kaylee directed Reese on where to put all the various plants. They lined up in a row beneath the mounted trophies on the study wall.

"You're not going to hang any ornaments or garland on these?" Reese studied a stuffed elk's head and its wide span of antlers, then stretched out his arms. "I could do it for you. I think I'm tall enough to . . . just . . . reach." He made a grand show of standing on tiptoe and straining to touch the antlers.

"Goodness, no!" Kaylee laughed. "All right. Let's get the bases set up. I hate to sound like Duncan, but I just might change my mind about some of my ideas once I actually see everything."

She opened her project notebook and asked Reese to trim and cut the floral foam, then soak it in water. Good thing she'd brought a portable worktable for doing the bulk of the preparation here. There was no way she could have stored everything for the room design at the shop and worked on the displays there, in addition to her regular business. The third-floor storage room already stayed quite full with her basic supplies and inventory for day-to-day business.

Kaylee turned to Reese. "I should check on Meghan to see

if she needs help with anything. Can you handle this for a bit?"

"No problem. Just let me know what I should be doing."

Kaylee left Reese in the study with specific instructions and her notebook, grateful to have a friend she could trust with such an important task.

She found Meghan in the narrow hallway between the great entry hall and the rear door of the mansion. Meghan, too, had brought a worktable and was busily stripping thorns and leaves from long-stemmed red roses. Buckets of them lined the hallway, along with buckets of green button mums, ferns, and white lisianthus.

"Hi, Meghan."

"Hey." Meghan barely glanced up from her work, and her deft movements with the knife never faltered. "I've got a lot to do today."

"If you need an extra pair of hands—"

"No, you've got your own displays to complete," she snapped. "I can't be pulling you off your work. Then neither of us will get things done in time."

"I have someone helping me, but if you're sure . . ."

"Yes, it's all right," Meghan said, her tone softer this time. "I can finish it on my own."

"I'm sure you can, but please let me know if you need anything. I'll be in the study." As Kaylee made her way back to her own room, she realized that Meghan had a good reason for turning down help and finishing the design by herself. She could use the execution of Kris's design in her portfolio, if not the design itself. This event could be added to her résumé. *Clever.*

"How am I doing?" Reese held up the floral foam.

Kaylee grinned. "It looks good. We're going to place the foam into this set of pottery vases. The silver ferns will go in here, along with the pinecones on stems—use one of each color in a bunch.

If you're not sure, everything's right here in the notebook."

She'd planned for three different table arrangements throughout the room, in addition to the runner on the coffee table, the display on the mantel, and two massive pillar candles on tall columns, one on each side of the hearth, wrapped with greenery.

The sconces flanking the fireplace would also be decorated with evergreen boughs dotted with red and green balls. They were a permanent part of the room and wouldn't be up for auction, but she didn't want to leave them undecorated.

In the corner stood a Norfolk Island pine, ready for decorating with ornaments and garland, and accented by a hand-quilted vintage-style tree skirt made by Orcas Island's own Deputy Robyn Garcia. The tree skirt had been the inspiration for the entire room. Kaylee had asked that Robyn's name be included in the description for that display.

"There you are." Barbara strode into the study. She wore a black pantsuit, and her white pearls encircled her neck. "You've barely gotten started, I see."

"Yes, but I have help." Kaylee motioned to Reese.

He waved at Barbara, who gave him a dubious once-over.

"Well, please make sure to do your best work," Barbara instructed. "We're counting on each and every display and decoration to bring in the most money possible."

"Of course. I have high hopes for all our arrangements. How is your room progressing?" Kaylee asked.

"I'm nearly finished with the tree in the dining room. Next, I'll see to all the displays. I've brought additional supplies to put up a display in the kitchen." Barbara cocked her head. "Have you heard from Mr. McTavish yet? I thought he would have started on the parlor by now."

"No. He told Mary he'd stop by the shop this morning to pick up his order."

"He'd better show up." Barbara shook her head. "Especially after nearly getting the entire event canceled because of his shenanigans."

I thought it was almost canceled because a man died, Kaylee thought, but she kept it to herself. "I hope he shows up, because the first floor of the mansion's decorations just won't be complete without his design in the parlor." Kaylee was still dubious about the use of tropical plants in the formal sitting room, but she wanted to give Duncan's design the benefit of the doubt.

"Key West Meets North Pole definitely wouldn't have been my idea," Barbara commented, then assessed the mantel. "Are you sure the supports are adequate for the forms? I'm afraid it might fall over."

Kaylee didn't miss Reese rolling his eyes in the background, and it helped her keep her voice cheerful. "I'll be sure to double-check them. Thank you."

"If you hear anything about Mr. McTavish, please let me know immediately. I should have known something like this might happen. And remember, I want us all out of here by six at the latest so I can lock up." Barbara spun around on her heel and marched back into the entry. Then her voice rang out. "Meghan, are you certain the top of the tree has enough ornaments?"

"Goodness." Kaylee sank onto an empty wingback chair and picked up her phone to check the time. It was nearly a quarter to one. She called Mary to ask if she'd seen Duncan.

"No, he hasn't been by to pick up his supplies, and he hasn't called either," Mary told Kaylee. "Have you heard from him at all?"

"No, I haven't. I was hoping he was on his way here." She glanced at Reese. "If he doesn't get there soon, then he won't have much time to finish his setup. And we need to be out of the mansion by six, per Barbara."

"Well, you wouldn't want to antagonize her," Mary said

with a chuckle.

"How's Bear?" Kaylee asked. "And how's everything at the shop?"

"Bear is happy as can be. He's napping as we speak," Mary said with a laugh. "It's been quiet, so I've been able to get the bows done for the pews at the Thompson wedding next week."

"That's good news. I'll stop by the shop when we're done here." Kaylee ended the call and sighed. "I would try to call Duncan's cell phone, but I'm not sure I'd get a response since no one else has. I think he's staying at Northern Lights Inn." She dared not verbalize her fear that Duncan had skipped town and wouldn't be here to take care of his design as promised.

"Call the inn," Reese suggested. "If he hasn't checked out, I'll head into town and pay him a visit."

She made the call, and the desk clerk confirmed that Duncan was still a registered guest there but refused to give Kaylee his room number.

"Could you please put me through to his room?" Kaylee asked.

The clerk complied, and it rang at least a dozen times.

The call cycled back to the front desk. "Ma'am, I'm afraid Mr. McTavish isn't answering. Would you like to leave a message?"

"Yes, please let him know that he needs to call Kaylee Bleu as soon as possible." She gave the clerk her number. "Thank you." She ended the call and set down her phone.

"If Duncan's in his room, he's not answering," she told Reese. "I can't get his room number, so even if you drove over there, they probably wouldn't tell you either."

"I'll bang on every door if you want." Reese's eyes twinkled.

"Thank you, but no." Kaylee thought for a moment. "But you *can* go over to The Flower Patch and pick up all of Duncan's plants and supplies and bring them here."

"Why?"

"Because even though Duncan isn't here to take care of his design, we can pull his room together if we can get enough people to pitch in. And whatever we have left over, we can use to decorate the ballroom. It won't be as fancy or elaborate as some of the other designs, but at least there will be something to bid on."

"That sounds good." Reese pulled his truck keys from his pocket. "I'll be back soon."

Kaylee had just completed the finishing touches on the study when, true to his word, Reese returned less than an hour later with the supplies for Duncan's design.

"There's still no word from Duncan, so this is on us," Kaylee said as she helped Reese unload the back of the truck. "No way will I let all this go to waste."

Of course Duncan had given her a small deposit to purchase the supplies he needed for his room, but Kaylee imagined she'd likely end up with the rest of the bill—all the more reason to put the flowers and plants to good use.

"What is all of this?" Barbara asked as Kaylee carried a box of ribbon and floral tape into the mansion.

"Duncan's supplies," Kaylee answered.

Barbara glanced out the front door. "And where is Mr. McTavish?"

"I have absolutely no idea. I've tried to reach him without success." Kaylee toted the box into the parlor and looked around. The spinet in the corner would provide a perfect base for a display. A corner chair by the window could be shifted to make room for the palm tree. *A palm tree, for heaven's sake!*

"Unacceptable. I suppose we'll have to put this together without him." Barbara's lips sealed into a thin line.

"We will, and it'll look fine." Kaylee marched over to the bookshelves. If they moved a few of the books, they could tuck a small display in the nooks the space created.

"I can help too," Meghan said as she entered the parlor. "It's two o'clock. If we need to be out of here by six, that doesn't give us much time to do this room."

"It's not much time for only one of us, but if we each take something, it can be done quickly." Kaylee headed for the entryway, passing Reese who was carrying a potted palm tree.

She could hear Barbara's exclamations of dismay all the way to the truck, and she tried not to laugh. A set of poinsettias in a box was easy enough to lift out of the truck's cab, so she brought that inside.

The next hour was a flurry of ribbon, wire, round Christmas balls rolling across the floor, and more exclamations from Barbara alternating with snippy comments from Meghan. Duncan had chosen a color scheme of hot pink and lime green, a play on the traditional Christmas shades of red and green, with gold as a metallic accent.

It wasn't half bad, Kaylee mused, as she considered the display she'd just assembled for the spinet. The crowning flower was a bird of paradise that oddly didn't seem out of place in the least.

Barbara spent her time directing everyone in logistics until she realized the others would be showing her up if she didn't make her own arrangement to decorate the room. She created a simple yet striking display for the mantel, complaining all the while that Duncan was letting everyone down, especially the students.

By the time the rooms were completed, Kaylee was more than ready to call it a day.

Barbara shooed them all out and locked up the mansion. "I've been notified that the owner has installed new security cameras," she told them. "I understand the old ones haven't worked in ages, but after recent events, they purchased a digital system. All the cameras are installed, so our work will be safe overnight." She appeared a bit wistful as she spoke.

Kaylee trudged out to her Escape, looking forward to a relaxing night at home with Bear.

Reese was waiting for her beside his truck, which was parked next to her vehicle. "Want to grab a bite at O'Brien's?"

"No thanks. I'm exhausted. A quiet night and an early bedtime are calling me." She glanced down at the space between their vehicles. There on the pavement was a pearl necklace.

Reese looked down too. "What's this?"

"It's Barbara's necklace. She always wears it." Kaylee picked up the pearls and scanned the lot. Barbara had already left. "Oh well, I guess I'll give it to her tomorrow."

She hoped Barbara wouldn't panic about it in the meantime.

16

On Friday morning, Kaylee decided to drop by Barbara's place to return the necklace. From this point on, the weekend ahead would turn into a blur and a whirlwind. She didn't trust herself to remember to return the necklace with everything else going on.

She pulled up to the curb and parked in front of Barbara's home, a Craftsman-style house in an older area of Turtle Cove. It was nestled on a quiet street not too far from the water. In fact, Kaylee could see the sparkling waves from the driveway.

She studied the house. It didn't seem to fit Barbara's personality. If she had to picture a home for Barbara, it would be something more palatial or a plantation-style home complete with Corinthian columns. Large trees flanked the house, which had a porch with window boxes and a wooden swing just right for two.

She looked over at Bear in the passenger seat. "I'll be right back."

Bear sighed.

Kaylee knocked on Barbara's front door, trying not to peer through the sheer curtain hanging in the window as she did so.

Footsteps sounded inside, and then she heard the click of a lock unlatching. The door opened. "Oh, Kaylee. What brings you here?" Barbara wore some type of terry-cloth turban in a shade of hot pink that matched her bathrobe.

"I wanted to drop off your necklace. I found it in the parking lot last night. Did you miss it?"

"As a matter of fact, I did." She opened the door wider. "Please come in out of the cold."

"My dog's in my car, so I should get going."

"Well, bring him in too." Barbara smiled. "I love dogs."

Kaylee returned to the vehicle and opened the passenger door. "Come on, Bear. You've been invited inside."

Bear yipped and jumped out excitedly.

They both headed up the sidewalk, then stepped into the house's entryway. A wooden staircase led to the second floor. She found herself standing on a bright blue rug. And froze.

Was it the same shade of blue as the strand she examined from Kris's boot? Was it only her imagination? Surely Nick had already questioned Barbara. The woman was devastated by Kris's death. Or she seemed to be.

Kaylee needed to find an excuse to get a thread from that rug. It wouldn't be admissible by itself, but if she got the sample and could compare it to the others found on Kris and the bush at the mansion, she might have something.

Suddenly Bear began rolling around on the rug, yapping.

"Bear, please stop." Kaylee turned to Barbara. "I'm sorry. He's usually not like this."

"No worries. He's adorable."

Kaylee finally convinced Bear to stop, and he plunked down next to her feet.

"I'll make us some tea," Barbara said. "It'll only take a few minutes."

Kaylee started to object, then thought better of it. Barbara motioned for her to follow, so Kaylee complied, Bear trotting next to her.

They entered a formal sitting room. In one corner stood an elegant Christmas tree, decorated with snowflakes and velvety balls in shades of slate and blue. A large fireplace framed by built-in bookcases was the focal point of the room. A fire popped and crackled. It was the perfect place to relax on a wintry day.

"Sit down. I'll be just a moment." Barbara ambled out, presumably to the kitchen.

Kaylee set her purse on the floor beside the sofa facing the fireplace, and Bear curled up next to it. She went over to examine the titles on the bookcases. Several interior design books, a few classics, and recent best sellers graced the shelves. Kaylee noticed a few mementos from Barbara's travels around the world. Each memento had a corresponding photo of Barbara with a rather distinguished-looking man. They'd both aged well, with photos reflecting their travels over the decades.

"Christmas hasn't been the same since my husband died," Barbara said as she reentered the sitting room. She held a tray that bore a steaming cup of tea with a little glass honey pot and a miniscule dish of sugar cubes beside it. Barbara set the tray on the coffee table.

"I'm sorry to hear that. He was a very handsome man. How long has it been?" Kaylee took a seat.

"Five long years. I feel like I've been at a standstill, and yet time has marched on without me. Without him." Barbara shook her head. "Kris was my answer. He got me moving again. And now, I have nothing."

"The memorial on Wednesday was very touching," Kaylee said. "I think he would have liked it."

"We were going places. He promised me." Barbara sniffed. "We were going to have an amazing show and travel the country, if not the world."

"You were going to be on the show too?"

Barbara shrugged. "I was. Those producers think they know so much. Kris and I had talked about the show extensively. Where we would go and who we would help. That's why the first episode was both lovely and painful to watch. I should have been there right beside him."

"That had to have been very disappointing for you," Kaylee remarked.

"It was." Barbara glanced at the tray. "I brought honey and sugar for your tea. I wasn't sure how you took it."

Kaylee picked up the cup and swirled some honey into the steeping tea. "Thank you."

"I was the head of the design club in school, heading to New York one day. That's why I was adamant about the tree auction being a success. It gives kids a chance to succeed. Like I wanted to."

"But you're successful here in the islands. I've seen your portfolio."

"Thank you. But I always wanted more. I wanted the opportunity that Kris was bringing to my life. Now it's all gone. He's gone." Barbara let out a pensive sigh. "Have you heard from Mr. McTavish since yesterday?"

"No, I haven't," Kaylee answered.

"I can't believe he would leave us in the lurch like this," Barbara moaned. "We all had to work our fingers to the bone to decorate his room."

"I've got his floral bill too."

Barbara clucked her tongue. "No accounting for lowlifes and slackers. Oh, I called the police department last night and let them know he's gone missing, that there were a lot of people depending on him."

"And what did they say?" Kaylee asked.

"That he's an adult, and right now there's no reason to think it's foul play." She rolled her eyes. "He could be halfway to Tokyo by now."

"Tokyo?" Kaylee repeated.

"It's a figure of speech. He just looks mighty guilty to me. I wouldn't be surprised if he's run off because his girlfriend is in trouble and they'll be looking for him next."

Kaylee nodded slowly. She almost admitted that she'd wondered the same thing. One other stop she'd make today was to see if Duncan was still checked in at Northern Lights Inn.

As she and Barbara chatted, Kaylee kept thinking about the rug in the entryway. Surely there had to be a way for her to get just a tiny tuft. Then she could give it to the sheriff's department so they could see if it matched the thread that was found on Kris's boot.

Her full attention was jolted back to the conversation when she heard Barbara say, "Will Sierra be able to get out of jail somehow? Do you think the sheriff arrested the right person?"

Kaylee considered her words carefully before responding. "I don't really know the answer to either of those questions. If they arrested her, they had to have found probable cause."

"There are plenty of guilty people who never get charged with a crime, all because no one can find the right evidence," Barbara said. "But in this case, who can argue against a $500,000 life insurance policy? Sierra must have been bitter, spending all those years without a father, and then she found out that there he was, living the good life a mere ferry ride away on the mainland."

At that moment, Kaylee's phone buzzed. "I'm sorry, but I should probably check that. It could be Mary at the shop." Looking at it, she found that it was in fact Mary letting her know she was opening the shop.

"Go on if you need to. It's a busy time of year for you." Barbara rose.

"Thank you for the tea," Kaylee said as she stood and collected her purse.

"You are most welcome." Barbara walked Kaylee and Bear back to the entryway.

Kaylee reached into her purse for her keys, which caught on something, and then most of the contents of her purse spilled onto the bright blue rug.

"Oh goodness." Kaylee sank to her knees on the rug. "I'm so sorry." She reached for a stick of gum, followed by a package of breath mints, lip balm, some stray pocket change, a handful of pens that had somehow ended up in the bottom of her handbag, and a few floral pins. She scratched at the rug. Was it enough to catch a strand or two under her nails? Would the silly ploy even work?

"Oh, don't worry about the mess," Barbara told her. "This rug has seen lots of wear and tear over the years. I've been meaning to take it to the cleaner, but I've been so busy. I plan to get it out of here after the weekend is over."

After raking in her purse's contents and putting everything back inside, Kaylee stood. Her fingernails felt as if she'd scraped up tons of grit. She hoped that there were some fibers among that grit. "Well, I guess we won't be seeing you as much when the House of Christmas Trees is over."

"I'm sure I'll see you around after tonight," Barbara said.

"Again, I'm very sorry about Kris."

"Thank you, dear."

Kaylee said good-bye. She couldn't get out of the house fast enough. She just *knew* Barbara was staring at her hands, that the woman could see the miniscule strands of wool rug clinging to the inside of her nails. And Bear? His decision to roll on the rug had been quite odd. She tried to slow down so she didn't look like she was trying to escape, and so Bear's little legs didn't struggle to keep up with her long strides.

After leaving Barbara's she drove straight to the sheriff's department in Eastsound, taking the chance that Nick would be there or someone who could help her remove any threads. No, they couldn't use these particular threads in court. She knew enough about investigative procedures to know that much was true. A warrant would be next, she guessed. But if there was a chance that Barbara might be literally getting away with murder, she had to throw doubt on the case against Sierra. If the threads didn't match, then so be it.

When Kaylee and Bear entered the sheriff's department, Aida greeted them.

She sat behind the front desk as usual. "Let me guess. You're here to see Deputy Durham." She popped a mint into her mouth, the other mints rattling inside the plastic container she held.

"You guessed correctly."

"Well, he's off-duty today."

Kaylee glanced around the empty reception area. "Is there someone else who can help me? I may have some information on a case that really can't wait. Maybe Deputy Garcia?" She didn't intend the note of urgency that crept into her voice, but there it was. How could she go around the rest of the day without her fingernails being checked?

"Good morning, Kaylee. What brings you by to see us?" Sheriff Maddox stood in the doorway.

"I have some information on the Kristopher Carroll case that might help you." Kaylee thought Sheriff Maddox would probably laugh at her. Maybe it was a useless quest. But deep down, she knew Sierra hadn't done it.

"Come on back. Let's talk for a minute, and I'll see if I can help." He motioned for her to follow.

As Kaylee walked through the reception area, she noticed a sign that said it was currently visiting hours at the jail. Perhaps a brief visit with Sierra would be in order after her meeting with Sheriff Maddox.

He led her into his office and closed the door. "Please have a seat."

Kaylee sat down across from the sheriff, and Bear settled at her feet. The sheriff's desk was neat as a pin except for a notepad, a pen, and a small box labeled *Death by Chocolate*. The idea of the sheriff having a sweet tooth made her smile inwardly. Until the first time she'd seen him at Jessica's shop, she never would have guessed it about the man. Sometimes you never knew about people.

Which was what led her to this errand today. You never knew.

Sheriff Maddox picked up his pen. "Tell me about this information you have. I'm all ears."

Kaylee took a deep breath. "One of the samples I examined from the scene was a blue thread taken from the bottom of Mr. Carroll's boot. A few days ago I found blue threads in a rosebush at the mansion, and Deputy Garcia is checking if they match the one from his boot. Today I believe I found similar blue threads in a rug."

"I see." The sheriff tapped his desk with the pen.

She held up her hands. "I'm hoping there's a bit of the blue thread from the rug under my nails. If so, I want to see if it matches the one found on his boot."

When the sheriff didn't say anything else, Kaylee realized how silly she probably looked, holding up her hands for him to see.

"So where did you get these threads—if any—under your fingernails?" Sheriff Maddox asked.

"I stopped by Barbara Lang-Masters's house today. The rug is in her entryway. It's bright blue. She mentioned that it's old and she's planning to send it out to get cleaned soon." Kaylee didn't tell him about Bear's strange reaction to the rug. She felt foolish enough as it was.

"That's very interesting." He stood. "I'll get some sample bottles along with a pair of tweezers, and we'll see what you have there."

"Thank you."

Sheriff Maddox paused in the doorway. "I can honestly say

that I've never heard of anyone trying this before. I can't promise you anything, but I'll ask Deputy Garcia to examine the strands as soon as possible. She's one of our go-to individuals in our criminal investigation section, although plant taxonomy isn't her specialty, like it is yours."

"Yes, that's why I don't feel comfortable trying to compare these fiber samples myself," she admitted. "Wool is a natural fiber, but it's definitely not plant-based."

He nodded, then headed out into the hall.

Kaylee turned back around in the chair, feeling better now that Sheriff Maddox hadn't completely dismissed her idea. If she was right, it could possibly make a world of difference for Sierra Underwood.

The sheriff returned, carrying a plastic vial, tweezers, and latex gloves. He set everything down on his desk except for the gloves. "This will just take a moment," he said, donning the gloves. He picked up the vial, removed the cover, then slid the tweezers beneath the edges of her fingernails.

"It looks like I'm picking up something here." Sheriff Maddox dropped the strands, tiny though they were, into the vial, repeating the gesture with every fingernail he swiped. "I'm sure we're collecting a lot."

Kaylee bit her lip. She typically kept her hands and fingernails very clean. Who knew what might be under her nails besides the threads? "Whatever it is, I hope it's useful in some way."

The sheriff finished with the last fingernail, then put the lid on the sample container. "As I said, we'll see." He peeled off the gloves and tossed them into the trash.

"I appreciate it," Kaylee said. "I noticed that it's still visiting hours. Would it be possible for me to talk to Sierra before I go?"

"We can arrange that. Of course, it'll be up to her if she'd like to see you." Sheriff Maddox stood, motioning toward the door.

"Thank you." Kaylee left the office, and Bear walked along beside her.

In less than fifteen minutes, a deputy came to fetch her from where she waited in the sheriff's department reception area. Aida assured Kaylee that Bear would make a great office pal for a while, and Kaylee followed the deputy.

Kaylee was escorted to the visitors' area at the jail. Soon she and Sierra faced each other across a wooden table in a room with other inmates also receiving visitors.

Sierra's hair hung limply past her shoulders. Her face was pale, her eyes shadowed. "Thanks for coming to see me." She grimaced. "They didn't seem to believe me when I told them I had no idea about the life insurance policy. Not really."

"What do you mean, not really?" Kaylee gently asked.

"The night of the reception, Kris said he'd named me the sole beneficiary of his policy. I told him to undo it, cancel it, whatever he needed to do to stop it. I didn't want his money. But he insisted. He begged me to let him make up for the past by ensuring I was taken care of in the future. He got quite upset when I refused."

"Ah, I see." That explained the altercation Mary had witnessed at the reception, the night Kris died.

"When he got upset, I got upset. Kris told me not to be stubborn. He said he hadn't helped me when I was growing up, but he wanted to make sure that if something happened to him I never wanted for anything again."

"Oh, dear." Kaylee sighed. "But of course the police didn't believe you."

"Why should they?" Sierra frowned. "Kris wasn't around to ask, and all I could do was tell them what I knew. But there was no one to back me up."

"Do you have any news about when you will be released?"

Kaylee asked.

Sierra's frown deepened. "No. But my attorney is hoping the bond reduction hearing will be this week so I can at least be out for Christmas."

"I hope so, and I hope it means you'll be out for good." It was on the tip of Kaylee's tongue to ask about Duncan's whereabouts, but she realized Sierra likely didn't know. And now probably wasn't the best time to tell her about his no-show and all that had followed yesterday.

"Everything's ready for tonight, isn't it?" Sierra looked hopeful for the first time since she'd sat down at the table.

"It is. The night's going to be perfect," Kaylee said, crossing her fingers.

Kaylee told Jessica about her surprise sleuthing adventure later when she stopped by Death by Chocolate for a cupcake. She'd left Bear at The Flower Patch, with a promise to take him with her after she was done for the day—and maybe a turn around the dog park, as the sun had warmed things up that afternoon.

"Sheriff Maddox himself scraped under your fingernails for samples of the rug?" Jessica sat on the edge of her stool in the office. "I can't imagine that. How soon do you think they'll know if the rug samples are a match?"

"I'm not sure, but he said he was going to ask Deputy Garcia to get right on it. If there is a match to the threads, I imagine he'll get a warrant to search Barbara's house. I know they want to wrap this case up, even though they've already arrested Sierra. I'm surprised he listened to me since they're trying to build their case against her."

Jessica rested her chin on her hand. "Of course, if this lets Barbara—or her rug, rather—off the hook, then it won't look any better for Sierra."

"I know, and that's what worries me a little. I don't want to make things worse." Then Kaylee thought of Bear's odd behavior. "As soon as Bear entered the house, he started rolling around on the blue rug and yipping. It was so strange."

"I wish I could have been there to see your face when he started doing that, let alone when you saw the rug."

"I was shocked. So was Barbara when the contents of my purse spilled all over the floor."

Jessica chuckled. "Did you find anything out about the video?"

"No, I didn't think to ask," Kaylee admitted. "I was in such a hurry to get my fingernails taken care of that it didn't cross my mind."

"I hope Nick calls you about it."

"He might now. I mean, they already have Sierra in custody. But I'm hoping her lawyer can get her bond reduced. She wants to be out by Christmas."

Jessica frowned. "Unless something dramatic happens, I don't see how that could be possible."

Kaylee considered something for a moment. "I wonder if anyone's heard from Duncan."

"I have no idea."

"I think I'll stop by Northern Lights Inn and see if he's around," Kaylee said. "Maybe he'll respond to a call that someone is actually there to see him."

"He might. If he's there, let me know what kind of explanation he gives for not showing up yesterday." Jessica shook her head. "It really burns me up."

"I'll keep you posted." She took her cupcake and one for Mary and returned to The Flower Patch, where Mary was assisting a customer and Bear was taking a nap.

When the customer left, Kaylee handed Mary one of the cupcakes. "How's it going?"

"Thanks," Mary said, unwrapping the treat. "It's pretty slow. Nothing I can't handle." She took a bite. "Mmmm."

"So you're okay if I do some more running around?"

Mary waved her away. "Go do whatever you need to."

Kaylee hugged her, then asked Bear, "Want to go for a ride?"

He leaped up and raced to the door, then glanced back at her, his tail wagging.

They made the short drive to Northern Lights Inn. It was a clean, comfortable place with a nautical theme.

Kaylee parked the Escape and headed inside, with Bear along beside her. There was lots of blue and white with hints of gold, and anchor and ship's wheel motifs were sprinkled throughout the lobby.

The desk clerk, a thin, balding man, looked up from his paperwork when she entered the lobby.

"Hello." She smiled at him. "I'd like to see if you could call one of your guests for me."

"What's the name?"

"Duncan McTavish."

"I'm sorry, but he's already checked out. First thing this morning."

Outwardly, Kaylee felt a jolt of shock, but deep down, she wasn't surprised. "Did he mention anything about any problems during his stay?"

"No, he didn't. Actually, I'm trying to reach him now, because his credit card has been declined. Do you know him?"

"Not very well," she said. "Only since he's been in town. I've been trying to contact him too."

"The only thing he gave me is his cell phone number."

"That's all I have as well. He does have a website, but I'm

not sure where his office is located."

"I'll find it. Thanks anyway." The clerk returned to his paperwork.

Kaylee and Bear went back to The Flower Patch for the rest of the afternoon. When they closed, Kaylee decided to take Bear to the dog park. A nice walk and some fresh air before the auction tonight would do them both some good.

Something told her tonight could be quite eventful.

17

Kaylee stood in front of the mirror and studied her reflection. The auction was set to start in a little more than an hour, and she was trying not to feel antsy about it.

She wore a dress, something she didn't do in her normal course of day-to-day life. But this evening she represented The Flower Patch and also her grandmother, so she figured it would fit the occasion. The black dress had a classic A-line skirt, it looked fancy, and most importantly, it was comfortable. She topped the dress with a cashmere cardigan that accented her eyes.

Bea had loved the photos Kaylee had sent her of the display in the gentleman's study. She called not long before Kaylee left for the open house and auction.

"It's beautiful. You've come into your own, and everyone will see how talented you are in your own right."

Kaylee felt herself blush. "I learned it all from you. I couldn't have done this without you."

"I can't wait to hear how much money you raise. I'm so, so proud of you." Warmth radiated through the phone, and Kaylee felt herself wrapped in a virtual hug.

"Thank you, Grandma. I'm almost ready to go."

"Is Reese picking you up tonight?"

"No. I'm driving myself."

"Ah, okay. Just asking."

Kaylee laughed. "You know I'm not really looking to meet anyone."

"Oh I know, dear."

She gave up discussing the romance in her life or the lack thereof. "What about you? Have *you* met anyone new lately?"

"No, missy, I have not." Her grandmother sounded amused. "There's an older gentleman who began attending the crocheting club not too long ago. I think he's just looking for someone to cook for him, as much as he talks to everyone about eating and all the splendid recipes he likes. He does know how to crochet a passable pot holder, though."

"Maybe he's lonely."

"Could be. I'm too busy to be lonely."

"That's good to hear."

"Well, I'll let you go. I know you need to get ready. Not that you'll have to do much to look beautiful tonight."

"Thanks, Grandma. I'll let you know how everything goes."

"I'll talk to you again tomorrow. It'll be bedtime here for me before too long. Time for a cup of tea and another chapter in my book."

Kaylee smiled as she fastened one of her favorite pieces of jewelry in place, a simple silver leaf pendant accented with her birthstone. She wore her hair down, simply styled, and used eye shadow, eyeliner, and mascara tonight. Her excitement about the event gave a natural pink hue to her cheeks.

"No muss, no fuss. Time to go." She slipped on low-heeled black pumps that completed her outfit.

Kaylee promised the ever-loyal Bear that she'd be home as soon as she could, and she also promised him some quiet time on Saturday. Then she headed out.

The designers had been given reserved parking spots in the corner of the mansion's parking lot. Snow had fallen that afternoon, creating a thin blanket of fresh white powder. *Definitely Christmassy.*

Kaylee took the rear steps of the mansion, where the

designers had been instructed to enter ahead of time, and then they were to take their places in their decorated rooms. After guests toured the mansion, taking in each of the rooms with numbered displays and decorations up for sale, the auction would start.

Barbara was in her element, helping to corral people and send them toward the auction registration table. When she noticed Meghan and Kaylee, she motioned for them to join her in the kitchen. "We get to go through the buffet line first," she said, "before they open the doors for everyone else."

They descended on the spread that included smoked meat along with an assortment of cheeses and crackers. A savory selection of appetizers and other finger foods covered the rest of the table. Over at the dessert table, Jessica had sent a variety of decadent cupcakes and bite-size treats, along with a chocolate fountain as the centerpiece with fresh fruit and chunks of cake to dip into the rippling stream.

Then the evening began in earnest, with guests filling the mansion's rooms, examining the displays, and noting the ones they wanted to bid on. The large crowd included people from the community, some Kaylee didn't recognize from the island at all, and several news reporters and photographers.

And there were photos, lots of photos. Kaylee lost count of the number of times people asked her to stand by the Christmas tree. A few others asked her to step aside so they could take a picture of it. Either way, she didn't mind. It seemed like the House of Christmas Trees open house and auction was the biggest event in the San Juan Islands that evening.

Kaylee's face ached from smiling, but she couldn't help standing a little taller and straighter as her work received compliment after compliment. A number of people asked about her grandmother and The Flower Patch.

She scanned the crowd and caught sight of Mary and Herb, Jessica and Luke, and DeeDee and Andy with their daughters, eight-year-old Polly and eleven-year-old Zoe.

Kaylee rushed over to them. "You made it!"

"I thought we'd never get to this night," Mary admitted, then enveloped her in a hug.

"There were times I wondered too, but here we are." Kaylee smiled.

"Oh, Kaylee," DeeDee gushed. "You've done an amazing job. I already know what I want to bid on." She nudged Andy. "I hope you're ready to spend a little money for a good cause."

"Uh, I think so." He grinned at his wife's enthusiasm.

Jessica leaned closer to Kaylee and lowered her voice. "Have you heard anything about Sierra?" she asked.

Kaylee had told her friends about her visit with Sierra in jail. She wondered about Sierra's bail reduction hearing and figured if it had happened, it hadn't gone well since she hadn't heard from her. "I haven't learned anything new."

"Her attorney came into the bookstore today," DeeDee said. "He felt confident something was going to happen, but he wouldn't tell me what."

"That's interesting," Kaylee said. "I certainly hope so."

"It's still a crying shame about Duncan, though," Mary observed. "But I've seen the parlor and the display in the ballroom. They both look fantastic, no thanks to him."

Kaylee shrugged. "It had to be done. I'm glad we were able to pull it off." She realized that Barbara hadn't even addressed the fact that Duncan wasn't present this evening. A few people had asked Kaylee, and she told them Duncan had left that morning.

Then Barbara raised her hands and announced, "Ladies and gentlemen, our auctioneer has arrived. Bidding will commence in ten minutes."

At last the auction began, being called by an auctioneer from Seattle. Kaylee was thrilled to see the kitchen's Christmas decor—a last-minute addition by Barbara—go for several hundred dollars for each of the three arrangements.

Next up was her room. The gentleman's study decor raised nearly $2,000, with $750 being paid for the Christmas tree alone. Her grandmother would be thrilled. Kaylee could barely contain her own excitement.

"Let's move to the dining room," the auctioneer said. "We have another Christmas tree, a table runner and displays, three wreaths, and a curio cabinet that was not originally part of the room, but it would make a nice display for collections."

As they trooped to the dining room they walked through the mansion's entry, where Kris's display would be auctioned off last. To think of the grand Christmas tree as *breathtaking* wasn't an adequate word. Its tip, where an antique star glowed with LED lights, soared past the top of the railing.

Meghan had decorated the entire tree herself with the use of a stepladder and some deft maneuvering while standing on the landing where the two staircases met. The tree's ornaments glittered in classic shades of red, green, and gold, with crystal icicles catching the shades of the ornaments and the clear lights beneath everything else.

The stair railings had real pine garland, giving the entryway a festive fragrance. On a small square table, close to the door of the closet where Kris had been found, a black-and-white framed photo of Kris stood. His eyes were closed, his head was tilted back, and he was laughing. Looking around, Kaylee saw that she wasn't the only one moved by the heartfelt arrangement.

Kaylee glimpsed a flash of headlights outside in the parking lot. A latecomer. But a latecomer in the form of a sheriff's office vehicle. *That's curious.*

Sheriff Maddox and Nick Durham entered the mansion. Nick gave Kaylee a serious look.

She joined them where they stood in the doorway.

"The fibers you picked up from Mrs. Lang-Masters's rug match the thread on Mr. Carroll's boots and the one you found in the rose garden," Nick told her. "We have a search warrant for Mrs. Lang-Masters's home. We're here to ask her to come in for questioning."

Sheriff Maddox nodded at Kaylee. "Good job."

Several people shot inquisitive looks their way, and someone murmured about the sheriff's office coming to bid on decorations for the department. A few light chuckles sprinkled across the room.

As they all filed into the dining room, Barbara hung back.

Kaylee guessed she was debating about whether to claim a spot in the front of the room where all the attention would be on her or to talk to the sheriff and the deputy and satisfy her questions about why they had shown up at the auction.

Barbara approached them, her curiosity seeming to win out. "Good evening, Sheriff, Deputy." She smiled. "I hope you'll enjoy some of the buffet. You're welcome to get an auction number if you see something you'd like to bid on."

"Thank you, but we're not here for a social call." Sheriff Maddox turned to Nick, who pulled out a folded paper from his pocket.

Kaylee glanced around. No one else seemed to notice the conversation taking place. Most had filed into the formal dining room where the auctioneer was extolling the features of each of the displays Barbara had designed.

"Mrs. Lang-Masters, this is a search warrant from the judge," Nick said. "We have permission to search your home in connection with the death of Kristopher Carroll."

Her hands fluttered to her necklace. "My house? Whatever for? I thought you'd arrested someone already."

"We did." The sheriff's voice remained low. "However, Mr. Carroll was dead before he was shot. That sidetracked us for a bit until we received the cause of death."

"Oh my. I thought he'd been shot. So then the gun didn't kill him?"

"No," Nick said. "We'd like you to come down to the station tonight. We want to take your fingerprints and get some hair samples."

Barbara swallowed hard. "Well, I can't come tonight. I'm too busy, as you can see." She looked at Kaylee. "Tell them it's impossible tonight with the auction, and we must secure the house afterward, and—"

"Please come with us now." Nick touched her arm. "We don't want there to be a scene. I'm sure you understand."

Barbara pulled away from Nick's hand. "All right, I'll go with you. But, please, I beg you, let me stay for the rest of the auction. I must see how much Kris's decorations go for. It's his last work ever. I need to witness it."

Sheriff Maddox exhaled slowly, as if considering her words. "We'll stay, and you'll stay near us like a fly on flypaper. But after this is over with, you'll come with us quietly. We're already dispatching deputies to your house."

Barbara gave Kaylee a pleading look.

But there was nothing Kaylee could or would do to help her. She still had plenty of questions, but at least it appeared Sierra's days in jail would be over very soon.

They entered the dining room, where the auctioneer made

quick work of selling Barbara's decorations. A businessman from Seattle purchased the whole lot for $1,200.

"Thank you, thank you," Barbara told the man as the room applauded.

Now it was time for the last display of the evening. The atmosphere in the mansion crackled with anticipation as they filed back to the entryway to auction off Kris's design.

"Here is a display called Classic Christmas, designed by the late Kristopher Carroll," the auctioneer said. "Reserve bid starts at $2,000 for the lot, but if someone is interested in an individual item, we will entertain bids if the lot does not sell first."

The front door burst open. "I bid $5,000!" a diminutive, gray-haired woman with black horn-rimmed glasses bellowed as she strolled into the entryway.

"Ma'am, you must have a number to bid." The auctioneer peered at her over the top of his reading glasses.

"It's Estelle Bentley," Meghan whispered, her skin turning a shade similar to the woman's hair.

So *this* was the whirlwind Kaylee had conversed with the previous morning? She couldn't help but smile at Estelle, who seemed to fill the room with her small figure. Evidently their conversation had spurred the woman into action for some reason. Was it loyalty to Kris? Or her interest in a good cause? Either way, Kaylee was glad she'd called Estelle. It was thanks to Duncan McTavish, rascal that he was. Wherever he was.

She idly wondered if Duncan's departure had something to do with the visit from Nick and Sheriff Maddox at the auction this evening. What if something had happened to him as well?

"Well, someone please fetch me a number, then." Estelle put her hands on her hips and regarded the room. "I'm not too late, am I?"

"No, not at all." Barbara stepped forward. "I'm Barbara Lang-Masters—"

"If you can't give me a number so I can bid on this display, I don't care if you're the Queen of England," Estelle snapped.

"Here's a number." Jessica waved a rectangular piece of white cardstock with a number printed on it and holly leaves and berries decorating one corner. "Your name, please?"

"Estelle Bentley of Portland."

"Ms. Bentley of Portland, you're more than welcome to bid." Barbara looked as happy as Bear did when Kaylee gave him a new bone.

The bidding then commenced on Kris's display, with Estelle Bentley the lone bidder. The Christmas decor went for the $5,000 she bid.

"Sold to number 125, Ms. Bentley," the auctioneer called out.

The room erupted into applause. It was the crowning moment of the night.

Kaylee wished Kris had been able to see it.

"Time to go, Mrs. Lang-Masters," the sheriff said quietly.

Barbara nodded, and the three of them began to make their way to the door.

All the while, Kaylee also observed Meghan sidling along the edge of the crowd, as if she were trying to keep out of someone's line of sight.

"Don't you skulk away, young lady." Estelle pointed at Meghan. "Your craftiness aside, I've seen your work. Sure, you learned some things from Kris, but who wouldn't after so many years with him? I can tell you have your own talent and a good eye. You don't need to ride on anyone's coattails. If you own up to your mistakes, I might have a job for you after all."

"You might?" Meghan sounded hopeful. "Ms. Bentley—"

The front door to the mansion opened again, and in strode Sierra Underwood.

Kaylee gasped.

Sierra wore a charcoal-gray pin-striped pantsuit with a white lace blouse and heels, her hair in an elegant updo. She nodded at Kaylee and Jessica.

"She's out," Jessica whispered, nudging Kaylee in the side. "And what a way to make an appearance."

Barbara, along with her police escort, had reached the door. She glanced over her shoulder to glare at Sierra, then turned to Sheriff Maddox. "That woman—"

"This woman made bail somehow." Sierra scanned the room as murmurs ran through the crowd. "Someone helped me. I don't know who, but I'm extremely grateful. Where's Duncan?"

"No one knows. He seems to have disappeared," Kaylee said.

Sierra frowned. "I don't understand. The other night Duncan said he was going to meet me. I know I'm late, but he insisted he'd be here for the auction." She walked to the parlor and peeked inside. "Where is he?"

"Hey, get back here!" Nick Durham shouted as Barbara slipped out the front door, then broke into a run. In a flash he was out the door after her.

As he followed, Sheriff Maddox hollered into his radio, "Suspect on the move!"

Kaylee and a few others stampeded out the doorway behind them and stepped onto the columned porch to watch. The photographers elbowed through the rest of the crowd, shooting photos of Barbara Lang-Masters hightailing it toward the woods. Kaylee reflected that it was a good day to be a reporter in Turtle Cove.

Someone else—Kaylee glimpsed a uniformed person with a ponytail—was in hot pursuit, arms pumping. Robyn Garcia. It was clear that Barbara, who was older, less active, and running in heels, didn't stand a chance of outrunning the much younger, fitter deputy.

Not thirty seconds later, Deputy Garcia returned, leading a handcuffed and limping Barbara along the driveway toward the mansion.

One of Barbara's shoes was missing a heel. Smears of mud and melting snow covered the front of her clothes. Her face looked like she'd been applying a mud mask. Tendrils of her platinum hair clung to one cheek.

"I'm not saying a word until I speak with my lawyer," Barbara huffed.

More flashes from cameras. Reporters shouted questions.

Yet somehow, despite the chaos around her, Kaylee felt truly at peace for the first time in days.

18

Despite the tumult surrounding the House of Christmas Trees open house and auction from start to finish—including Kris's death, followed by Sierra's arrest, then Barbara being taken away in handcuffs after trying to flee the mansion—the event was well attended and brought in more than enough to keep the scholarship fund going for several years, with a few recipients each year.

The phone rang at The Flower Patch "for the umpteenth time," as Mary put it the following Monday morning. "I'm about ready to beg you to hire someone just to answer the phone and respond to the same questions every single caller has been asking," she grumbled as she went to answer it.

Somehow word had gotten out about Kaylee Bleu, the florist and plant taxonomist who had played a role in helping the sheriff's department ferret out the truth behind the evidence that pointed fingers firmly at Barbara Lang-Masters, despite her efforts to plant evidence that would lead to Sierra.

Kaylee grinned. "Maybe we should put a sign on the door for FAQs."

Mary stuck out her tongue and picked up the phone.

The Petals had decided to gather this morning to discuss everything that had happened over the weekend. Sierra, now released from jail and completely cleared of any charges, would join them as an honored guest.

"Would you look at this? We're front-page news," Jessica said as she entered the shop. She waved a stack of newspapers. "I found the island papers, and it's in the Seattle and Portland news too. Estelle Bentley must be a big shot down there."

"Let me see." Kaylee took one of the papers and perused the article.

When DeeDee and Sierra arrived, they all gathered in the consultation area with coffees provided by Jessica.

Once everyone was settled—Mary near the phone—Kaylee shared what she had learned. "Barbara was reeling with jealousy that Kris had left her out of his show. I'm still not sure if the production company nixed Barbara as being part of the team or if it was Kris's doing." She sipped her chocolate latte. "Whatever the case, Nick believes Barbara wanted to get back at Kris in the only way she could—ruin his involvement in her own show here on the island."

"Except that didn't work the way she hoped." Sierra frowned. "Kris told her about me, and she was looking for any way she could to discredit me. I already knew she doubted Kris was my father—or at least, she wanted to. But I really don't think she planned to kill him and had to scramble to cover it up."

Kaylee nodded. "Kris's death was completely accidental. The way Nick explained it to me is Kris had told Barbara he didn't feel well, and she told him to go back to her place so she could take care of him that night. When she got home after the reception, Barbara gave Kris a cup of tea. She'd laced it with sleeping pills. The thing is, he'd already taken some of his own medication that interacted with the sleeping pills. Giles Akin believes Kris keeled over from an overdose that caused heart failure."

Sierra picked up the story. "Barbara knew about my gun, so she broke in, stole it, and shot Kris, then used the rug to tote him back over to the mansion when the coast was clear. There wasn't much blood because he was already dead when she shot him. She told Nick that the overdose was a complete accident, and she panicked. Her grief was very real."

"She's also the one who left me the notes," Kaylee added. "Her fingerprints were on both of them."

"Whew, that is a *lot* to do in one night." DeeDee shook her head. "But how did Barbara get into the mansion without breaking in?"

"Well, first she had an extra key made," Sierra said. "I figured that out when Kaylee told me Barbara insisted on locking up at the mansion on the day I was taken in for questioning. I was surprised when Kaylee mentioned Barbara had a key, because I thought I was the only one dealing with the mansion's owner. I was kind of miffed that Barbara had gone ahead and gotten a key too. You know, since she can never seem to keep her fingers out of the pie, so to speak."

"That explains it," Mary said. "But why would she hide the body in the mansion?"

"That's a good question," Jessica answered. "I don't see why she didn't just take a boat out and dump him. So much easier."

"Ooh, I wouldn't want to get on your bad side." DeeDee nudged her fellow Petal playfully.

"Maybe she was so far gone emotionally that she wanted Kris to be found in the last place he created something beautiful. That sounds silly too. I don't know." Kaylee shrugged. "I can't fathom what she was thinking. Anyway, Nick said her lawyer is going to try for involuntary manslaughter instead of first-degree murder. They can't argue away the obstruction of justice charges, though, among other charges."

"How did you make bail?" Mary asked Sierra.

"That was thanks to Estelle Bentley. She and Kris were close friends for years. She told me she thought of him as a brother. She put up $50,000 to get me out of jail. She gets it all back now, thank goodness." Sierra sighed.

Then she sat up straight and tapped on an end table. "I have an announcement, ladies. I wanted to let all of you know that Kris really was my father. Even though my mother sent him a letter, we did a paternity test to make sure. He didn't want to say anything to Barbara right away, because the mere hint of what she considered a complication would set her off. He really did love her. He just hadn't figured out how to handle her. Which is why he hadn't actually proposed yet."

"She had me wondering for a bit," Mary admitted. "Barbara has always had a bit of a flair for the dramatic, so I figured it was Barbara being, well, Barbara."

"I think she had all of us wondering," DeeDee said. "But toward the end, I was sure Duncan had something to do with it, the way he disappeared like that." She turned to Sierra. "I'm sorry."

Until now, no one had brought up the elephant in the room that was Duncan's disappearance from the open house and apparently Orcas Island altogether.

The phone rang, and Mary hopped up to answer it. "I bet that's another reporter. Or the bride for the wedding this weekend."

She returned a few moments later, looking a bit flustered. "Kaylee, I hope you don't mind, but I just hung up on a customer."

"Why's that?" Kaylee asked.

"It was Duncan McTavish, ordering a dozen roses for Sierra. He wanted to apologize," Mary blurted out. "I couldn't see him trying to buy off an apology."

"I don't blame you," Kaylee said. "The nerve of that guy."

"His card would probably be declined." Sierra rolled her eyes. "I don't want flowers from him, anyway."

Sierra's phone rang. She glanced at it and made a face. But she tapped the screen. "Duncan, why are you calling me?"

His voice came over the speaker. "Because you deserve answers about what happened."

She stared at the phone. "Go on."

"I'm a jerk. I didn't mean to be. But Barbara had me in a corner. Kris had dirt on me, which he shared with Barbara. He had a recording of me threatening him, which she played for me. She said if anything ever happened to him, she'd make sure the authorities came looking for me."

Kaylee and the others sat on the edges of their seats, listening.

"Well, that's interesting." Sierra's tone was flat.

"Barbara played the recording for me that night, and she made me help her move his body," Duncan said. "But I didn't want to. It ruined everything. I should have come clean to begin with. I . . . I really liked you."

Sierra cleared her throat. "I really liked you too."

"I'm coming back to Orcas to turn myself in. I already told the sheriff and got a lawyer. But I wanted you to hear it from me first."

"Thank you, Duncan."

"I hope you can forgive me someday."

"Me too," Sierra said. She ended the call, then looked up. "That explains a lot."

"It most certainly does," Kaylee said, thinking back to the morning Duncan had confronted Barbara in the shop. He'd likely been eaten away by guilt even then. *That's why he told me to talk to Estelle. He knew she'd help.*

"Well," Sierra said with a smile, "thank you, all, for everything. It's good to have friends like the Petal Pushers."

At that, Kaylee thought of something and stood. "My fellow Petals—and Sierra—let's take a moment to make something here in the shop. It doesn't matter what it is. Pick a vase or a pot for a plant. I want each of you to have something beautiful to take home with you after this roller coaster ride we've been on the past couple of weeks."

"Oh, Kaylee." Sierra's voice quivered. "Thank you. I feel so foolish now, thinking about Duncan and what he pulled. I should have seen it coming."

"What exactly happened with you and Duncan?" Mary asked gently after they assembled in the workroom at the table, now covered with pots and plants, floral foam and ribbons.

"Oh, I was so silly," Sierra said. "Duncan and I had been in contact before he came to Orcas, so we already had a casual friendship before he got here. He irritated me, especially with the animals at the mansion stunt. Then after Kris died, he intrigued me. I knew he and Kris had a past, that they never saw eye to eye. So I started finding out everything I could about Duncan McTavish. Then somewhere along the way it seemed like he noticed me. It happened fast. And, well, the rest is history."

"He really was concerned about you after you were arrested," Kaylee said. "He talked to me about it the day of the memorial."

Sierra snorted. "I bet that's because he was worried it would make him look suspicious. Somehow he got wind of the life insurance policy. He confessed to me that he was almost broke and asked me for a small loan."

"It seems to me you should be thankful you escaped him," DeeDee told her, "just in time apparently."

"No wonder Oliver was so droopy." Jessica shook her head. "What a tangled web we weave."

"How's Oliver doing now?" Kaylee asked, grinning.

"Perfectly fine, with perky, happy leaves," Jessica reported brightly. "It's a definite sign. Smooth sailing until Christmas."

Kaylee raised the red ribbon she held. "To smooth sailing until Christmas and into the New Year."

"Hear, hear." Jessica waved her own ribbon before tying it around another geranium.

Kaylee surveyed her friends as they talked and laughed. She

would still miss her family on Christmas, but she was thankful for times like this with friends who were like family. It was a glorious season in Turtle Cove.

Bear woke Kaylee early on Christmas morning. It wasn't as if he knew Christmas was a special day. Or did he?

The dog followed Kaylee to the coffeepot and did a little tap dance on the kitchen floor, whining.

"Hold on, Bear. It's a bit chilly this morning. Let me get your coat."

He gave a yip, then scratched at the back door.

"All right, we'll skip the coat. But don't say I didn't warn you," Kaylee said as she let him outside.

She took a moment to enjoy the beautiful morning. Traces of snow remained under a clear blue sky.

When Bear raced back inside, Kaylee poured a cup of coffee, thinking about her morning plans. She would open the gifts sent by her family and call to thank them. Likely they'd already be finished with breakfast and her nieces would have unwrapped piles of presents.

As much as she would have loved to be with them, Kaylee didn't regret staying in Turtle Cove and not flying to Florida to be with the rest of the family. Maybe she could visit them next Christmas, but this year, it was important to keep her grandmother's business going.

She smiled at the thought of her grandmother. What did she have planned for Christmas Day? They hadn't really discussed it. Perhaps she was still dealing with the changes her own big move had brought to her life. No doubt her sister would make sure she had the perfect Christmas.

Her phone rang. Jessica.

"Merry Christmas!" she said to her friend.

"Merry Christmas to you too." There was a lilt to Jessica's voice this morning. "Have you had breakfast yet?"

"No."

"Good. I'd like to bring your gift over and some breakfast too."

"Oh, that's sweet of you. Thank you. Does breakfast involve anything chocolate?"

"Maybe something like chocolate chip pancakes to go with fruit, omelets, and homemade cinnamon rolls."

"That sounds delicious. Give me a chance to get dressed, and come on over."

"I'll see you in about twenty minutes. Is that long enough? Luke is still conked out, and we're not eating until around two. You're welcome to come over for dinner. We're having surf and turf."

"I'm heading to Mary and Herb's this afternoon, but thank you. I'll see you soon." Kaylee ended the call, then ran to change into a comfortable sweater and a pair of jeans.

Jessica pulled into the driveway exactly fifteen minutes later. *Someone is sure excited about Christmas morning.* But then, Kaylee's stomach growled in anticipation of something more than a bagel with flavored cream cheese for Christmas breakfast.

The passenger seat was occupied. Kaylee strained to see who it was. *Wait a second—*

"Grandma!" Kaylee jammed her feet into her slippers, then flew out the door and down the front steps of Wildflower Cottage.

As soon as Jessica stopped the car, Kaylee's grandmother unbuckled her seat belt and threw open the door just in time to embrace her granddaughter.

"Oh, how I've missed you!" Bea said, squeezing Kaylee.

Happy tears pricked Kaylee's eyelids as she hugged her

grandmother. "And I've missed you. Merry Christmas." She stepped back, grinning at her. "I can't tell you how surprised I am."

Bear danced around their feet, yapping excitedly.

They all laughed.

"Well, I'm glad my surprise worked," Jessica announced. "I told you I'd be bringing your Christmas present over." She nudged Kaylee's elbow. "Go on inside. I'll get your breakfast fixings."

"I couldn't stay away," Bea said once they were inside the cottage's snug and warm kitchen and sipping cups of coffee.

Jessica stood at the stove, whipping up something for breakfast. She had refused their offers to help, insisting that they sit and catch up.

"I'm so glad you didn't." Kaylee hurried to the living room and grabbed a large flat box on the coffee table. It contained something very special, something she hadn't yet mailed out to Arizona with the rest of her grandmother's gifts. She returned to the kitchen. "Because now I get to give you your Christmas present in person." She held up the box. "Merry Christmas, Grandma."

"What on earth?" Her grandmother wasted no time opening one end of the box. Kaylee helped her place it on the table, and Bea slid out the painting, wrapped in foam. She peeled back the layers, then clamped her free hand over her mouth. "Our Flower Patch. Oh, Kaylee, you shouldn't have."

"I didn't. It was a gift from the artist. He insisted that you have it, and he's sending me a print for the shop."

Bea enveloped her in another warm hug. "Oh, my heart is full. I'm so proud of you, Kaylee. I knew you'd do a great job with The Flower Patch. I'm loving life in Arizona, but I got to missing you and my friends, and I just had to come back for Christmas."

"The Petals will be so happy to see you." Jessica grinned at them as she watched from beside the stove. "In fact, I'll call a special meeting between now and New Year's Eve. The chocolate is on me."

Kaylee sipped her coffee and smiled at her grandmother and Jessica. Life was never dull in Turtle Cove, and she definitely looked forward to what the New Year would bring to Orcas Island.